Broken Chords

Barbara Snow Gilbert

I extend heartfelt thanks to my friend and fellow musician,
Peggy Green Payne.
—B.S.G.

Published by
Dell Laurel-Leaf
an imprint of
Random House Children's Books
a division of Random House, Inc.
1540 Broadway
New York, New York 10036

ISBN: 0-440-22887-5

RL: 7.0

Reprinted by arrangement with Front Street Books, Inc.

Printed in the United States of America

April 2001

10 9 8 7 6 5 4 3 2 1

OPM

It was the same polished pink granite foyer Clara had crossed twice a week since she was three years old and began lessons in the old music building, so familiar she didn't see it anymore. But this time something stopped her cold: the ponytail, neatly brushed and bound collar-high with a green rubber band. The person to whom it belonged had his back to her as he studied the bulletin board. A new column of numbers had been posted—the reading scores.

Her soles clicked on the stone, but he didn't turn around. A worn leather backpack hung off one shoulder; initials were tooled into the flap at her eye level. MHL. The monogram was simple and neat, but the tool had slipped in a couple of spots, as if he might have done the work himself.

"Hi," she said from behind his back.

He did not turn around. Maybe he knew she was there and was mad. He might have a right to be. She wasn't sure who had mixed up the music, and the incident had probably cost him some points.

The Five Owls described Barbara Snow Gilbert's highly acclaimed first novel, *Stone Water*, as "an intensely moral coming-of-age story, which effectively shows that some of life's most serious questions have no one answer; each person has to grapple and find his or her own point of resolution." Barbara Snow Gilbert is an attorney with extensive experience in litigation and mediation. She lives in Oklahoma City with her family.

ALSO AVAILABLE IN LAUREL-LEAF BOOKS:

THE HERMIT THRUSH SINGS, *Susan Butler*
BURNING UP, *Caroline B. Cooney*
ONE THOUSAND PAPER CRANES, *Takayuki Ishii*
CHINESE CINDERELLA, *Adeline Yen Mah*
MIND'S EYE, *Paul Fleischman*
TIME ENOUGH FOR DRUMS, *Ann Rinaldi*
THE SPRING TONE, *Kazumi Yumoto*
NOBODY ELSE HAS TO KNOW, *Ingrid Tomey*
TIES THAT BIND, TIES THAT BREAK, *Lensey Namioka*
CONDITIONS OF LOVE, *Ruth Pennebaker*

to my daughters
Stephanie and Allison

Long ago on the plains of Russia, there lived an old man and an old woman. Always they stood at their door, watching the children of the other huts play in the snow. One day the man said to the woman, "Let us make a little snow girl. Perhaps she will come alive and be a daughter to us." And so they put on their fur hats and coats and went out into the cold.

Tenderly, they fashioned the snow girl's arms and hands and fingers. And as they worked, her eyes began to shine as blue as the twilight, her lips to glow as red as the sunset. She smiled, and her hair flew behind her in the wind, and she danced, whirling like a snowflake and singing softly. The old couple watched and wondered and thanked heaven, and when night fell, they tucked the snow girl into the best furs and pulled her bunk closer to the fire.

At dawn, they rushed to pull back the covers, eager to see the bright eyes coming awake from sleep. But the snow girl was gone. As they cried out, the door blew open and a cold draft swirled through the hut. And the old man and the old woman heard clearly the words of the snow girl's song, carried behind her on the wind:

Old ones, old ones, I had to go
to my kin, of the snow.

"The Little Daughter of the Snow"
A traditional Russian folktale

First Movement

"Candidate fifty-two," boomed a voice from behind the judges' screen.

Clara pulled the mustard-colored Chopin book from her satchel, stood, and with perfect posture crossed to the nine-foot Steinway.

Her grace was an acquired trait, not a natural one, and she credited Tashi—Natalia Petrovna Volkonskaya, her piano teacher—for it. Four years ago, when Clara was thirteen, she had finally been allowed to begin ballet lessons. It was Tashi who had intervened with Clara's mother after years of overhearing her student's begging. "An understanding of the dance will strengthen an understanding of the music," Tashi had counseled, speaking in her formal English with only a trace of a Russian accent. Then Tashi had whispered to Clara, "Perhaps it will add that certain something." The whispered phrase had blown a cold chill through Clara. If something needed to be added, something must be lacking . . .

Clara handed her music to the page-turner and willed her focus back. Seated, she turned the knob on the bench to accommodate her five feet eight inches. She checked the pedal distance and action, making sure her soles made no noise. The seat was too close by an inch, but Tashi had a firm rule: no scooting. "A singer does not cough before an aria." Clara stood, lifted and reset the bench, then checked the pedal distance again.

It was important to get it right. This first weekend in October was known in music circles as the Second Cut, an unnerving stage of the Nicklaus Piano Scholarship Competition. Today consisted of examinations: a theory test, and the sight-reading evaluations now under way. The performance portion of the competition started tomorrow, when students presented their individual programs. Anyone here had already made it past the First Cut, based on recommendation letters from their teachers and taped submissions reviewed over the summer. Anyone surviving after this weekend would be one of five candidates going on to the finals at the end of November.

Clara floated her long silk vest out over her pants, an outfit her mother had brought home just for the occasion. The blouse underneath was sleeveless. Clara never wore sleeves when she performed, mostly because they got in her way, but also, she would admit, because she had studied the portrait in the hallway at home and she liked the way her strong, slender arms looked from the audience.

Although Tashi had a rule against wearing any ornaments—"The only sparkles should come from the music"—Clara had slipped in antique, slightly dangly, ruby earrings borrowed from her mother's jewelry box. Then she had brushed her hair back behind her shoulders, making sure the rubies showed.

The Nicklaus was an old competition, and the rules, as amended over the years to meet every contingency, were quirky. Because it had proven difficult for the committee to pick sight-reading music no entrant had previously studied, candidates chose their own music for the reading evaluation. They were allowed to play their selection through once beforehand to judge its suitability; enforcement of the once-only rule was left to the honor code, a pledge signed by both student and teacher. Ensuring a high score for the difficulty factor, Clara had picked a Chopin nocturne in D-flat minor with so many notes the pages looked more black than white. She wasn't worried about the notes, but she was worried about the acoustics. The testing was being done in several rooms of the university music building, and Clara had been assigned to a converted faculty lounge. She would have to work hard to get the rich, haunting melody the nocturne required out of a piano surrounded by plush rugs, upholstered furniture, and heavy drapes.

The page-turner took the extra copy of Clara's music out of the book and passed it behind the screen. Abruptly, Clara stopped thinking of the room and the rules and her clothes and the pedals and how it all looked and felt.

Arms in her lap, she listened for the slow, lento tempo inside her head. When she heard it, she gave a nod, and the assistant read from the paperclipped page. "Frédéric Chopin."

Clara placed her hands on the ivory and felt the keys arranging themselves under her fingers.

"Opus 34, Number 1. Valse Brillante."

Opus what? Valse what? Clara hadn't brought her Chopin waltzes. They were boring, with their endless one-two-three, one-two-three.

She stared at the pages the woman was setting in front of her. This music was in A-flat major. This music was in three-four time. This music was not her music.

It would do no good, but Clara couldn't help reaching up and turning back to the front cover. There was the trademark mustard yellow with the simple leafy border in which Schirmer's published all its library editions. There was the familiar CHOPIN in big black letters. There, in smaller letters under it, were the words "Waltzes for the Piano." Not "Nocturnes for the Piano" but "Waltzes for the Piano."

At presto speed, Clara searched her memory. She recalled sitting on the bench before the afternoon session. She had been going through her music satchel, looking for the Prokofiev she was playing in her program tomorrow. That boy with the blond ponytail—a man, really, he could have been twenty—had been sitting beside her. And there had been several mustard-colored Schirmer's books in his stack, too.

The page-turner cleared her throat. Clara didn't move. She was still staring at the cover. Under the title, in a quick, neat hand, someone had penciled in, "Reading Selection—Second Cut."

She turned back to the waltz. She could disrupt the proceedings, confess she had brought the wrong music, and refuse to play until her nocturne was in front of her. Or . . .

Well, she could handle a cold sight-read of a Chopin waltz. Even if it was as fast as vivace. The waltz might not be difficult enough to get the score she would have with her nocturne, but if she played cleanly she would do fine. The acoustics might be easier to overcome with a bright waltz anyway.

As if to hint that the wait had been too long, the page-turner picked up the corner, ready for the first turn. Clara took the line in at a glance and heard the lilting music in her head. It wasn't that bad, really. She would pretend she was dancing it. No problem. The problem would be for the guy with the ponytail.

It was the same polished pink granite foyer Clara had crossed twice a week since she was three years old and began lessons in the old music building, so familiar she didn't see it anymore. But this time something stopped her cold: the ponytail, neatly brushed and bound collar-high with a green rubber band. The person to whom it belonged had his back to her as he studied the bulletin board. A new column of numbers had been posted—the reading scores.

Her soles clicked on the stone, but he didn't turn around. A worn leather backpack hung off one shoulder; initials were tooled into the flap at her eye level. MHL. The monogram was simple and neat, but the tool had slipped in a couple of spots, as if he might have done the work himself.

"Hi," she said from behind his back.

He did not turn around. Maybe he knew she was there and was mad. He might have a right to be. She wasn't sure who had mixed up the music, and the incident had probably cost him some points.

It was not a small matter. The winner of the Nicklaus earned a four-year scholarship to the Juilliard School in New York City, and a debut New Year's Eve Concert with the local orchestra, the Oklahoma City Philharmonic, and the attention of the music world . . .

"Excuse me," Clara tried again. Adding a "sir" crossed her mind, but she quickly ruled it out. Even if he did turn out to be twenty, twenty wasn't a "sir."

Unable to think of other alternatives, she stepped closer. His shirt gave off a faint scent of spray starch, the kind her dad used to do the ironing. She tapped him on the back.

Under her hand, his shoulder blade straightened, and he turned around as she stepped back.

His green eyes blinked.

He had the scantest bit of a five o'clock shadow, which was unexpected because most of the boys Clara knew had nothing close to a five o'clock shadow. The stubble made him look as if he had spent the day at the beach and sand had blown up against his face—except that was wrong, because he hadn't been out in the sun in a very long time. The pale skin was reassuring. If there'd been even a trace of a tan, Clara wouldn't have believed he was a pianist at all.

He raised his eyebrows.

"I thought you might be looking for this." Clara brought up the Schirmer's and held it out to him.

"Oh. Gosh. Thanks." He slipped her book of nocturnes out of his backpack, studied the cover for a moment, and made the exchange.

Clara threaded the straps of her satchel through every single buckle. "I hope this mess didn't cause you too much trouble," she said, cautiously.

"Don't worry." He laced the flap of his backpack. "It's okay."

She almost smiled but caught herself. Instead, she tipped her head and angled her eyes up at him.

Clara had watched the girls at school leaning against the lockers, smiling and trading wisecracks with the guys going by. And Clara's friend Holly was queen of the flirts. But Clara had never done it, not even once. Now here she was, practically batting her eyelashes. She straightened and cleared her throat.

"Well," she said, striving for an offhand tone, "I'm glad I found you. So we could trade back," she added quickly.

"Sorry if I didn't notice you at first." He nodded toward the bulletin board, hesitated, then said, "It's my third try."

Clara couldn't think of anything to say to that. Because it was an undergraduate scholarship, the Nicklaus was only open to ages sixteen through twenty-one. The competition was held every other year, so three chances were all anyone got. God, he had put himself through this abuse three times?

She rechecked the buckles on her satchel.

He relaced the flap of his backpack. "Well," he said, shrugging. "Good luck."

"Well," she said, shrugging back. "You too."

A rusty Schwinn was propped next to the wall. He flipped the kickstand up with the toe of his tennis shoe and started to roll the bike away. But then he stopped and turned back around. Clara hadn't moved.

"I like your earrings," he said. "They're nice."

"Thank you," Clara managed to get out.

Hoisting the bike to his hip, he headed down the stairwell and called back, so that his words echoed behind him, "Nice nocturne, too."

Clara's jaw went slack. If she hadn't been on guard her mouth would have fallen open, though it wouldn't have mattered now.

Nice nocturne? Not difficult nocturne? Not you-ruined-my-chances nocturne?

She turned to the bulletin board and realized a crowd had gathered. Wedging herself between the bodies, she found "Clara Alexander Lorenzo" near the middle of the printout. She had already seen her first two scores: 100 for her taped submission, another 100 for the theory test that morning.

Quickly, she ran her eyes across to the new, third column, "Reading Evaluation." "Chopin, Valse in A-flat Major, 95."

She put her finger to the sheet and followed the line across again, making sure she hadn't gotten off by a space. She hadn't.

It was okay. As high as she could have made, considering that the waltz wasn't that difficult.

Her finger only had to move up one name to find an MHL. "Marshall Hammonds Lawrence." She traced the line across the page. "100. 100. Chopin, Nocturne in D-flat Minor, 100."

She watched her thumbs passing under, her fingers tumbling over, as her hands climbed up and down the keyboard, warming up for her lesson. Tashi said scales were tides, gentle and lapping, but with invisible powers. Clara thought of the image now as she watched her hands ebb and flow, toward and away from the crystal snow-globe on the ledge of the piano.

As long as Clara had studied, the snow-globe had been there. When she was small and had played especially well, Tashi would shake it and they would watch the snowflakes swirl around the Russian girl and boy, arms interlocked as they skated on the mirrored pond. Now that Clara was older, Tashi didn't shake the globe for her anymore, but she sometimes held it in her lap when Clara played, petting it like a kitten.

Shifting her fingers up a half-step, from the white keys of F major to the black keys of F-sharp major, Clara started the next ascent while Tashi finished a student consultation in the adjacent room.

Tashi was the only faculty member with a spacious office adjoining her teaching chamber, one of her perks as occupant of the Nicklaus Chair. The original Mr. Nicklaus had emigrated from Germany in time to stake claim to some of the richest mineral deposits in Oklahoma. Oil baron, college founder, and patron of the arts, he was married to a former Juilliard student, which was the source of the alliance between the two schools. It was a relationship that served both institutions well: the competition sent Juilliard promising pianists, and in return Juilliard loaned its faculty on teaching sabbaticals. It was how Tashi had first come to this university on the plains, and when she retired from Juilliard and her performance career, she moved back to stay.

The student left. Clara continued playing, but the muscles in her neck and shoulders tightened. Twice during the weekend Tashi had phoned Clara's house for updates, but drained from the Second Cut schedule, Clara had already been in bed. She wasn't sure exactly how much detail her parents had revealed.

"So how did it go, my darling?" Tashi called from the other room.

Clara turned her head to watch Tashi's reaction. "Okay, I guess."

Tashi stopped searching her sheet music files and looked at Clara over her half-glasses, the silver rims of which were studded with multicolored imitation gemstones. "Okay, I guess?"

Clara put her eyes back on her fingers and answered loudly enough to be heard over the four-octave crescendo. "My program was good. The Mozart and Prokofiev, fine. I thought they'd deduct on the Debussy because I got a little carried away with the pedal in the middle . . . but they didn't."

Tashi, dressed in a sequin-studded sweater, purple skirt, and red leather ankle boots, stood beside her. "And?"

"And"—Clara leaned to the left as she moved into the lower range of the keyboard—"and theory was a 100, and sight-reading was a 95." She had tried to slip it in unnoticed, but her timing was bad—the "95" fell right in the crack between the last low notes of F-sharp and the starting notes of G.

Tashi took her reading glasses off so that they swayed from the silver chain under the ledge of her ample bosom. "And so, my darling, did something happen?"

Clara had considered telling Tashi about the mix-up. But it might lead to telling about MHL. She had looked for him Sunday, wanting to hear his individual program, but he had played before she arrived. "Just lost my focus for a sec." In a way it was true. If she'd been focused she wouldn't have switched her music.

"You know, Tashi, sight-reading counts for zero, anyway. The judges fix the finals to make it come out however they want. Until the November playoffs all this prelim stuff is just a throwaway."

"And do *they* agree with you, Clara, that the preliminaries are, as you put it, a throwaway?"

"They" were Clara's parents. Vince Lorenzo, Clara's father, was a baritone soloist who had left the opera houses behind because it kept him from his family. He was the choral music director at Clara's high school and taught piano on the side. Clara's mother was Ellen Alexander, conductor of the Oklahoma City Philharmonic, the same orchestra that would debut the winner of the Nicklaus Competition. Clara often thought of her perfectionist mother as the Maestra because of an incident years ago when a fan called out, "Wonderful concert, Maestro!" Clara's mother had smiled and waved, but she had tightened her hold on Clara's fingers and whispered in her ear, "The correct title is Maestra, of course, when 'the master' is a woman."

When Clara had confessed the 95, the Maestra had closed her score without marking her place and grabbed her calculator. She kept statistics on prior winners and knew the formula for weighting the different phases of the competition.

"Five whole points?" She jabbed in numbers, figuring the scores Clara would likely need on her program selections, as she spoke. "When every decimal of a decimal counts?" Clara's father, sorting laundry, had sucked in his cheeks so that his salt-and-pepper beard caved in by an inch on both sides. His hands kept folding socks, but he was suddenly mismatching colors.

Clara attacked her final scale with a loud forte, intending to close the subjects of both her parents and the 95. Tashi sighed and settled into the straight-backed chair beside the bench, then propped a new piece of sheet music—a blue cover with a snowflake design—on the piano rack.

Good. That was the thing about Tashi. She knew when to move on, unlike the Maestra, who all weekend had dropped the 95 into every conversation.

Scales complete, Clara stood to lower the piano lid. On Mondays, the student before her always left it up, but Clara preferred it closed in the tiny teaching room. She laid the rack flat, then lifted the lid off the support and was slowly lowering it when the back of her elbow hit something smooth and hard and cold.

There was a splash of sharp, high keys and Clara looked over her shoulder to see the snow-globe rolling down the keyboard. She knew she should keep holding the piano lid. To let it fall would mean eardrum-breaking noise and possibly damage to the instrument—

Clara dropped the lid.

As crashing thunder and sound waves from vibrating strings overtook the room, Tashi's hands darted out. The crystal globe landed in their nest, then slipped free. Clara had fallen to her knees and elbows—knocking over the bench in the process—and now, in one huge, final effort, she slid her fingers along the floor.

Echoes of the shaken piano box died away and Clara realized the cold weight was in her hands. But one side of the snow-globe, she thought, had hit.

She stood up and made herself inspect the crystal: a hairline crack, visible only if you looked very hard.

Clara put the globe into Tashi's shaking, spotted hands, turning it to reveal the damage. Tashi studied the fracture, then lifted the crystal back to its ledge and collapsed into her chair.

The piano bench lay on its back; the new sheet music lay scattered. Clara wiped the dust from her hands and clothes, righted the bench, then kneeled next to Tashi, who sat with eyes closed and hands splayed across her chest. Clara put her arms around her teacher and said nothing.

"Dinner's ready in twenty measures!" Vince Lorenzo's baritone sang out from the kitchen.

In the music room, Danny, Clara's twelve-year-old brother, stopped bowing the squeaking string bass.

Clara pulled her soggy jogging clothes off and tossed them over the posts of her bed, where towels and book bags and T-shirts already hung from every knob. Clara detested jogging, it was so boring and regimented, but it kept her in shape for ballet. On crowded piano-lesson days, she ran only the bare minimum—a two-mile loop through her neighborhood—but she never, ever skipped.

She toweled off, then grabbed her school clothes from their puddle. As she dressed, she glimpsed pieces of herself in the full-length mirror. Hundreds of symphony tickets were stuck into the frame, blocking her view. She had collected them since she was little, her mother waking her up when the concert was over and carrying her backstage to get the guest artists to sign them. Dressed now, she maneuvered around the tickets and posed in first position.

Solid turnout. She raised her arms to fifth, and the frayed edge of her cropped-off long-underwear top rose above her blue jeans, exposing her midriff. Narrow waist, flat stomach. Good proportions for ballet—if only she weren't so tall. Her gaze moved up. A nice face wasn't essential for a dancer, but it didn't hurt. Dark eyes to match her brown hair, lots of lashes and brows. Skin she rarely had to deal with if she kept on a film of untinted Clearasil, and a shaker's worth of freckles across the bridge of her nose.

Then, carefully, she smiled.

And there it was—the thinnest bit of a space between her two front teeth. It was the reason Clara didn't smile much, and if she did, she tried to keep her lips together. Her dad refused to take her to the orthodontist. He said Clara's smile was her hold on one-of-a-kind beauty and he would not be a party to wrecking it. But Clara would have, in a minute. As soon as she was earning her own income as a concert pianist, the first thing she was buying was braces.

"Ten measures!"

Clara's parents took the dinner hour seriously. The Maestra broke orchestra rehearsals from six to seven-thirty just to be home, and everyone at the table was expected to talk. Well, tonight Clara was going to give them something to talk about.

Feeling for the papery crinkle in her pocket, she pulled out the Nutcracker brochure. She had made notes on the back, and now, one last time, she ran her eyes over the list of arguments.

"Five measures!"

The roar of Ellen Alexander's twenty-year-old Triumph convertible punctuated the announcement.

Clara folded the brochure back into her pocket, brushed her hair off her face—the way the Maestra liked it—and headed out her bedroom door.

There were only two bedrooms, both of which Clara's parents had given up, preferring a bed in a corner of the den to either of their children going without their own room. Clara's bedroom should have been the master, and was on the front of the thirties-style bungalow. To get to the kitchen, she had to go through the area that was intended to be the living room but which was, in the Lorenzo family, the music room.

Turning sideways, she edged around her mother's lacquered black Yamaha. The other piano, a seven-foot rosewood, was her father's. With their question-mark curves fitted back to back, the two instruments almost completely filled the room. The perimeter was taken up by metal shelves, crowded with the cut-out cereal boxes that her father used to organize the family's music. Clara's music was in the Wheaties section.

As usual, Danny had left his string bass leaning up against the shelves, blocking Clara's route, and she dropped to her hands and knees to crawl under the pianos. She had crossed the room this way since she was little, but this time she scraped her backbone on the exposed wooden ribs.

"Danny!" she shouted, though she was already past the roadblock. "Move your instrument!"

"One measure," Vince Lorenzo said matter-of-factly as Clara walked under the archway, rubbing her spine. He stood at the stove in a chef's hat Danny had ordered with coupons off a biscuit can, his eyes glued to the Mickey Mouse on his wrist. Pulling a string of spaghetti out of the pot, he dangled it.

Danny, who had been waiting for this, took the pasta and flung it against the refrigerator. The theory was, if it stuck, it was done.

Clara took her place at the table as her mother surged through the back door. "Sorry," the Maestra said between breaths, juggling her briefcase and a bulging day-planner. "The Mozart second movement needed a full run-through."

"Perfect timing, as usual," Clara's father said. "In right

after the pickup note."

Striding by behind Clara's chair, her mother bent to kiss the top of her daughter's head. "I don't often get to kiss that lovely head anymore."

Clara pulled away. She was too old for her mother to be kissing her, and the indirect reference to her height was annoying. Especially coming from her petite mother, whom Clara had passed in height and weight in the sixth grade.

Her mother hugged Danny, who was forming spaghetti into the shape of an interlocked "OU" on the refrigerator door and didn't look up. "These bangs have an appointment with my scissors," she said, finger-combing the tow-head strands, the tips still green from summer chlorine.

At last, Ellen Alexander turned to her husband. "Spaghetti. What a nice surprise." It was a joke. Clara's dad knew only seven meals, and Monday was always spaghetti. Being careful not to let her suit rub against the stains on his apron, she pulled him down by the neck and kissed him full on the mouth.

At the table, Clara's father said his usual one-sentence prayer expressing gratitude for their many blessings. The Maestra took the daily report—from Clara about her piano studies, from Danny about his school day. Finally past all the rituals, Clara handed her plate to her mother.

"Did you two know my ballet school is doing the Nutcracker this Christmas?"

Her mother filled Clara's dish and passed it back to her. "Of course we know, Clara." She reached for Danny's plate. "The symphony is accompanying."

"Well, sure. But what I bet you didn't know is, Madame has announced auditions."

Her mother's blue eyes widened. She had already ladled two heaps of sauce onto Danny's pasta, but she ladled on a third.

Clara angled herself toward her father. He would let her have her say, which would force the Maestra to be still and listen. And if Clara could win him over, he'd help with her mother.

"I know it's a long shot," Clara said, "but I thought I'd try out."

The ladle fell into the platter of spaghetti. Clara kept her eyes on her dad, took the Nutcracker brochure from her pocket, and slid it across the table. No one picked it up.

Her father finished pouring the wine, then set the bottle gently down. "When would rehearsals be?"

"Nights," Clara answered quickly. "And they wouldn't interrupt my lessons because they wouldn't start till late."

"But you'll be wanting extra practice time," her father said. "Won't you, Clara? Be wanting extra practice time?"

"I'll get it in."

"Get it in when?" He sounded worried.

"More than three hours a day?" her mother leaped in. As if Clara didn't know how long she practiced.

"Listen, both of you," Clara said, though she kept her eyes on her father. "I wouldn't ask to do anything that would jeopardize the competition. You know I wouldn't. But it won't be a problem.

"The Nutcracker will be a way to take a break from my

work. I'll need breaks, and it would be a nice diversion. The exercise will be a good thing. It will be important to stay healthy. My grades are all up. And besides, I do better at everything when I'm scheduled a little tight. If I ever do have to make up piano time, I'll practice longer in the mornings. Get up earlier."

There were lines between her father's eyebrows. "How much earlier can you get up than five-thirty?"

"Four-thirty," Clara answered quickly.

He stroked his beard. "A seventeen-year-old girl—young woman—cannot get by on four and a half hours of sleep. We already worry about you—"

"And the way you cram everything in," her mother snapped.

You are one to talk, Maestra, Clara thought. But she didn't say it. Or even look at her.

Silence hung over the table. Even Danny sat perfectly still. From behind the green bangs he stared at Clara. His mouth was full of salad, but he wasn't chewing.

"Sweetheart."

Here it came, the speech her mother had been organizing. Clara knew by the careful reasonableness in her voice.

"I know you like your dancing—"

Liked her dancing? Clara loved her dancing.

"—but it isn't anything you're ever going to go anywhere with, I'm sure you know this. And the Nicklaus is the opportunity of a lifetime, frankly, for a p—"

For a moment Clara thought her mother was going to say "prodigy." But words like "prodigy" and "genius" weren't often used in their house. Clara didn't know if she was a prodigy, but she was close enough that no one felt comfortable talking about it.

Without missing a beat, her mother started the sentence over. "And the Nicklaus is the opportunity of a lifetime, frankly, for a *person* with your gifts. We have been very reasonable, Clara. We've kept you in school. Put up with the ballet. But there are times for breadth and there are times for depth, and now is a time for depth. You should be cutting back on extraneous activities, not adding new ones. And not just because the Nicklaus means the best school and the best teachers. And not just because it opens career doors and goes at the top of your résumé. The Nicklaus is the opportunity of a lifetime, Clara—and I know that you know this—because it furthers your art."

Deep inside Clara, something began to shudder.

"Balance all that against the Nutcracker," her mother summed up, "and I'm sure you'll see. It's a silly comparison. The Nutcracker—it's . . . well, a Christmas show. A cliché."

A cliché. Apparently the worst thing the Maestra could think of to call it.

"And so what if it is?" Clara reined her voice back down and enunciated carefully. "I want to do it."

"Okay. Everyone take a breath." Her father, of course. Her father the mediator. "How about we sleep on it, talk in the morning?"

"I don't need to sleep on it," Clara said, eyes filling. "All I want to do is try out for the Nutcracker. It isn't the biggest deal in the world, but you two are turning it into that by saying no." She wiped her eyes.

"Actually, we haven't said no," her father pointed out.

"Well, your father may not have said no," her mother said, springing to close the opening. "But *I* am saying it, and right now, too. No." She picked up the brochure and held it out to Clara, but Clara didn't take it.

"I do not think it would be doing you any favors, Clara, to let you imagine for one moment longer that trying out for the Nutcracker is even remotely possible. It is not. You will see that eventually. In the meantime, I am sorry to disappoint you, very sorry, but I can't allow such a misstep."

Clara dropped her napkin by her plate. The wallpaper behind her chair was torn, something the Maestra constantly nagged her to watch out for when she scooted back. Now, she pushed away from the table hard, making sure her chair bumped.

Hoping to make her exit before the tears turned to sobs, she stood up and took the brochure from her mother's outstretched hand. She folded it and put it in her pocket.

"I need to be excused," she said, passing beneath the arch. She dropped to her knees to crawl under the pianos, then added, loud enough that they could hear, "From this family."

Books propped on her hip, Clara leaned against the auditorium wall. Usually she sat in the front and was one of the few kids in study hall to actually study. But today she had calculated a spare twelve minutes, and she was watching for Holly. It was the first time they'd had together all week.

There. The corkscrewing red hair, in a huddle of green cheerleading uniforms.

"Holly Nicole!" Clara yelled across the room.

Holly stepped out of the huddle, and her eyes found Clara's.

Clara waved, remembering the first time she had looked across a room into those startling turquoise eyes. It was the afternoon of her first ballet lesson, and Clara had just made a horrifying discovery: everyone else in Ballet I was six years old. Waiting for Madame to start class, Clara had clung to the wall, staring at the elastic on her shoes. That was when Holly had walked in. Now, four years later, they still stood side by side at the barre, still coupled every time Madame called partners. The Nutcracker was supposed to have been like that, too . . .

Holly put two fingers in her mouth and whistled back at

Clara, which was possible because her hands were empty. She kept a B average without ever taking a book home. Pointing to the back of the auditorium—away from the faculty spotters—she waved Clara up the aisle, and the two girls plopped, in unison, into the last row.

"I have bad news," Clara said, kicking off her sandals.

Holly fished a can of Cherry Coke out of her cheerleading bag, a canvas duffle covered with the autographs of her five hundred closest friends. She held the contraband under her seat and popped the tab. "Okay. So spill it."

Clara pulled her feet into the seat. Her overalls were worn through at the knees and she picked at the threads. "The Maestra said no to the Nutcracker."

Holly waved her off. "Jeez, Clara, the way you were sounding, I thought it was going to be something grim. Just tell her you have to try out. You're my ride to rehearsals."

"No, really. She's not going to change her mind, there's no way."

"Clara." Holly turned the turquoise eyes on her friend and spoke sharply. "There is always a way."

For Holly, it was true. To pay for her ballet lessons and cheerleading uniforms, she ran a spring-through-fall lawn-mowing business out of the back of her dad's pickup.

"Yeah, well." Clara sighed, and said, not unkindly, "Some of us have parents to deal with."

Holly's mother had left when Holly was two. Her dad had raised her, but he was a night watchman and never around.

"Oh, lighten up, Clara." Holly smiled, showing dimples.

"You'll figure something out." As if that solved it, she dug a box of Band-Aids out of her cheerleading bag, propped her Reeboks on the seat-back in front of her, and began bandaging the blisters on her palms.

Clara opened her chemistry book at the pencil—a chewed-off stub—and checked her watch. The equations were due next period.

"So how did your piano thing go?"

After Sunday's program scores were factored in, Clara had ended up in first place. She kept her head down, working. "Pretty well."

"Pretty well?"

"Okay, very well. And by the way, I meant to tell you." Clara stopped balancing the equations and looked at her friend. "I met someone." She would have called Holly about MHL before, but the Lorenzos' only telephone was in a niche in the hall in the middle of their house. "A guy."

A huge smile broke out on Holly's face and her eyes seemed to turn even more turquoise. Maybe it was the mascara; Holly hated her red lashes, and today she had loaded on navy blue. "A guy? I didn't think you even noticed which ones were guys."

"His name is Marshall." Clara couldn't resist adding, "He's older." She went back to the equations.

"How much older is older?"

"Twenty, maybe—"

"Twenty!" Holly's feet popped off the seat-back and she jumped around in her chair.

It shocked Clara to see her friend so surprised. They were

juniors now, but even when they were freshmen Holly had gone out with seniors.

"Okay, Clara. I want details."

"Well, he's nice. Nice looking and—nice."

"And . . ."

"Long hair." Clara tapped the toothmarked stub against the notebook paper. "Sandy colored. Wears blue jeans. And he plays. Of course."

"And . . ."

"And he's only four points behind me."

"And . . ."

"And that's it." Clara went back to her homework.

"No, it's not," Holly said bluntly, putting her feet back on the seat. "I could dig up lots of nice guys with long hair and blue jeans that can tink out a few tunes. What's so special about this guy, that he's the first one you even notice in seventeen years?"

Clara tapped her pencil again. "I don't know . . . He's, well, mature. And committed to his music."

"You're attracted to a guy because he's committed to his music?"

"Yeah. I think so."

"Clara, you are scary."

Holly dropped the box of Band-Aids into her bag and picked out two bottles of nail polish, one white, one green. "So, your parents, did they flip over your running with this older guy?"

"We're not 'running.' We just met." Envious of the long nails, Clara stopped working long enough to watch her friend spread on a layer of glossy white.

"Anyway," Holly said, laughing, as she moved on to the next fingernail, "guess your mom can't say much about older, can she?"

Clara hadn't thought of that. Her father was fifty-eight, fourteen years older than her mother. He was already an established opera soloist by the time he met Ellen Alexander, a student conductor at the Santa Fe Opera one summer. Holly was right, her mom couldn't say anything about age. Not that there was anything to say anything about right now.

"So when's your next rendezvous?"

"Competition finals. End of November."

"Jeez, Clara, November's a lifetime from now." Holly screwed the cap on and dropped it back into her junk. "I'll run through two or three guys between now and November." She started in with the green on her other hand. "Maybe you oughtta call him."

Clara had already ruled it out. She was carefully plotting her next encounter: let him see her at the piano, let him hear her play. "No," she said, "I'm going to wait him out."

Holly fanned her hands. "You must really like this guy if you're playing it this cool."

Good. She was playing it cool. Clara checked her watch and went back to her chemistry. Only a few more problems to go.

All through her next lesson Clara waited for Tashi to bring out the Beethoven Concerto Number 1 for Piano and Orchestra in C Major, the performance piece for the finals, six weeks away. But the clock ticked down almost all of Clara's two hours without the Beethoven appearing, and Tashi always left promptly at six. Six was when her Pomeranians, Johann and Sebastian, got their dinner.

Clara had studied the concerto briefly twice before, once when she was thirteen and again at fifteen. She hadn't cared for the piece, finding it easy and uninteresting, but she understood why the committee had chosen it—competitions were careful to pick music that wouldn't stretch young pianists too far too fast.

Nicklaus concertos were named far in advance, so of course Tashi had known all along that the Beethoven would be the audition piece the first year of Clara's eligibility. But Clara hadn't known. Now, she was worried that she had treated the concerto too casually on her first quick passes, and that it had been so long since she'd played the piece at all.

In the past few months Clara had asked Tashi over and over for the music. Each time, Tashi had taken her reading glasses off, looked Clara in the eye, and pronounced,

"Knead. Rest. Knead. Rest. The bread is still rising."

At her Monday lesson, with the Second Cut behind them and work on her individual program over, Clara had expected Tashi to at long last prop the concerto on the piano rack. But Monday had been the disaster with the dropped snowglobe—not a time to begin work on anything.

But today—today, Clara was finally going to get her music. She knew she was, because she was going to bar the door. Tashi would give the concerto to her if it was the only way she could leave to feed Johann and Sebastian.

Tashi's office clock chimed the first six notes of "Für Elise" and Clara eyed the door, wondering if she really had the nerve. When her eyes cut back, the frayed, eighty-one-page Beethoven score was in front of her.

Clara lunged for the music and hugged it to her. "Thank God." She flipped through the pages, running her fingers over the penciled-in fingerings, phrasings, and pedalings.

"Now that you two have greeted one another," Tashi said, holding her hand out, "I need the music back."

Clara hugged the concerto tighter.

"I promise, Clara. You and your music will go home together."

Dutifully, Clara handed the book over.

Tashi spent the next fifteen minutes with an art gum, removing all traces of the fading pencil marks. "And now, my darling," she said, blowing away the eraser dust, "you have never seen this music before."

Whatever. Clara could go along with Tashi's games as long as she had her music.

"Take it home, read it, copy the notes onto staff paper, build the chords out of blocks and knock them down and build them over, caress it, sleep with it if you wish, but"—she dangled her glasses—"do not play it."

Clara stared at her in disbelief. "But—"

"Nyet."

"But the finals are only—"

"Nyet."

"Tashi! You can't be serious!"

"Promise me, my darling." As if she were prepared to let Johann and Sebastian wait all night for their steak niblets, she crossed her arms over the music.

"Okay." Clara nodded weakly. "I promise."

Tashi put the concerto on the rack. Then she set the blue-covered sheet music that had scattered at Clara's last lesson in front of it. She tapped the snowflakes with her baton. "Play this instead."

Five thirty-two a.m. and Clara was the only one up. Nobody ever slept late in the Lorenzos' house. She was their alarm clock.

In the dark, Clara felt the way to her favorite of the two pianos, her father's rosewood, with curving legs and carved ivy and vines, brought over on a boat from Italy generations before.

The cold bench stuck to her thighs as she slid across. She was dressed in her dad's old undershirt, worn so thin it was barely there, and a stretched-out pair of ballet shoes. To keep them on, she had pulled on ragg socks with cut-out heels and toes that she used as ankle-warmers in dance class.

Palming the digital timer, she punched in three hours. She'd pause it when she stopped to get ready for school, and start it again that afternoon. The red numbers beamed out at her from the dark. She remembered wanting the time-keeper so badly—when she was nine years old she had used her birthday money to buy it. Now she regarded it as merely a necessity. It always told her exactly how many minutes she had left.

Clara positioned the timer on the ledge and opened the Beethoven to the entering piano solo. She was supposed to spend her usual three hours practicing, laying everything aside except exercises, "head work" on the concerto, and the new piece. Sighing, she ran her fingers over the first page of notes, then put the forbidden Beethoven back into her music satchel.

She pulled up the new sheet music. "The Little Daughter of the Snow," by Mikhail Maninov. Maybe she'd skip technique and do a read-through.

Clara opened the music and felt her eyes grow large. The treble clefs were giant swirls, the notes big black dots. She scanned to the double bar at the end. The whole piece couldn't have been fifty measures. As if there had to be more, she turned the music over. A children's story was printed on the back cover. Something about a little girl made out of snow.

God, Tashi. A fairy tale set to a kid's tune? Three hours a day of "head work" and a third-year student's recital piece?

Clara closed "The Little Daughter of the Snow." Without turning on the light—it hurt her eyes this early in the morning and she didn't need to see to practice technique—she began arpeggios, broken chords, running up and down the black and white keys which the early morning shadows had turned a monotone gray.

Tashi said arpeggios should be a brook skipping down stones, free and easy. Clara's felt anything but.

That night, after helping her mother with the dishes unasked—penance for what she was about to do—Clara rolled up her pale blue leotard with the silk demi-skirt, ballet shoes, pointe shoes, and her newest pink tights. Packing her dance clothes in the bottom of her satchel, she covered them with her music.

She had never revealed the date of the Nutcracker tryouts to her parents. Once her dad had put his arm around her and asked if they needed to talk more about it. Clara said no and ducked away. There was no hope the Maestra would change her mind, and it would be better to let them think she had accepted the ultimatum.

Now, standing by the kitchen door, Clara focused on the sponge under her mother's fingers and ignored the sick feeling in her stomach. "I'll be back by ten-thirty," she said. As if to let the music satchel do her lying for her, she held it up by the strap, her university ID protruding from the front pocket.

When Clara received her driver's license, Tashi had given her a special-status ID card to get into university buildings so that she could use the practice rooms. Understanding the need to work undisturbed, her parents encouraged the habit.

"Practice?" her mother asked, approval embedded in the question.

Clara shouldered the satchel and answered carefully. "Practice."

Tryouts took most of two hours. "Attention, ladies and gentlemen." Madame rapped her ballet stick on the floor, a list in her hand. "I have your parts."

The talking hushed. Clara and Holly had been stretching

at the barre, legs propped. Now they turned and faced Madame.

The solo parts had already been filled. Clara's hope was to make the corps de ballet as a waltzing flower or a snowflake or both. She crossed her fingers behind her back, embarrassed for anyone to see but figuring it couldn't hurt. Odd—she couldn't remember ever doing that before a piano competition, even when she was small.

Madame started with the waltz. Clara sensed Holly at her shoulder, also not breathing. And then there it was, right up front. "Holly Adamson."

Holly exhaled, blowing her bangs.

Clara gave her a thumbs-up and listened for the L's. But Madame went straight from Brandy Kelso to Hillary Macguire.

Finished announcing the waltz corps, Madame moved on to the snow scene. Holly's name was called. That was good. That was great. But now Madame was through the alphabet, and again there had been no L's.

They looked at each other from the sides of their eyes. They both knew what it meant. The ballet had parts for toy soldiers and rat warriors, but the little kids would get those because Clara was too tall. All that was left were the couples at the party in Act I.

Madame started the list of ladies, and Holly's name was called a third time. As the other names went by, Clara tightened her fingers and said a quick prayer. It was possible the list was out of order. Madame might have tacked her on at the last minute. The final ladies' part was announced. Not Clara.

Holly squeezed her arm, but Clara couldn't look at her. She put her eyes on the planks in the floor. If she counted the wooden pegs, maybe she could keep from crying. One. Two.

And then, "Clara Lorenzo," so quick she wasn't sure if she had heard it or dreamed it.

Her head bobbed up, but Madame had gone on. Clara turned to Holly, searching her face.

"The guests," Holly whispered.

"But they already called the guests."

Holly unclipped her hair. Her curls bounced and her turquoise eyes sparkled. "Not one of the lady guests, Clara. One of the men."

It was a disappointment, but a disappointment one step up from the disappointment Clara had thought she was getting. And it made sense. She was tall enough to pass for a guy. Probably they'd just walk around the stage, maybe dance a little minuet or something. But she'd be as good as she could be. And at least she'd be a part of it. Not a recital, a real ballet. A real ballet with an orchestra.

An orchestra. The orchestra. The Maestra conducting. So what was she going to tell her mother?

Fifteen days and five rehearsals later, Clara was still letting her music satchel speak for her as she headed out the door.

Madame called a break. Clara stopped stretching and peeked through the shutters that hid dance class from the rest of the world. People in business suits leaned into the wet autumn wind, hurrying home on a Friday evening. Clara especially loved ballet when it was stormy outside. The brightly lit room reflected in the mirrors and wood floors, the feel of her leotard stretching against her skin, the squeak of the resin . . . Ballet was its own perfect universe. At least, it used to be. Ballet didn't feel quite so perfect anymore.

Madame rapped her ballet stick and called Scene I. Clara took a place in the first row.

Usually in class Clara stood in the back, relying on the better dancers to help her remember the combination. But the minuet was so simple. Clara had forced herself forward, intent on earning a place front and center in the final blocking.

"Minuet, from the top." Madame's fluttering hands marked the steps, and Clara lifted her arms in preparation as the pianist began.

Pointe, pointe, pas de bourrée, hold while her partner turned . . .

Clara pulled herself tall and lifted, straining to make the lines of her body elegant.

Dancing shouldn't be a strain. But over the last couple of weeks, everything was beginning to seem like a strain. School. Homework. Piano practice. Even sleeping. All the things she usually ticked automatically off her list.

Pointe, pointe, pas de bourrée . . .

Was it the sneaking out? Or the stress of not being able to practice the concerto when she knew the other finalists' fingers were numb from practicing it? Other than technique, the only thing Clara had been playing was the Maninov. She felt silly because it was so simple. But she had to admit, the melody had grown on her.

Step, step, turn and bow . . .

It was a sad little song, with a minor beginning, major middle section, and minor finish. Sometimes Clara made up variations on its theme. Often she went to bed with the tune replaying in her brain. After this weekend, though, Clara doubted she would be playing the song anymore. Monday would be exactly four weeks from the finals, and Tashi had promised her, after midnight this Sunday, she could—

Jesus! Her weight was wrong for the turn and bow. She was falling, the floor flying up at her—

Clara's lungs chucked out their air.

The fluorescent lights flickered. A dull pain crept up her arm, which was pinned under her.

The pianist stopped Tchaikovsky mid-phrase. Over her,

faces gathered. One was Holly's.

Clara struggled to refill the bottom of her lungs. God, dancers—even bad ones—hardly ever fell to the floor. Much less during a minuet.

Breathing again, Clara stood up slowly. But as soon as she moved, the dull pain became a nauseatingly sharp one, shooting up through her right arm and shoulder and the side of her neck.

She clenched her jaw. Madame walked around her in a tight circle, tapping her ballet stick.

"I'm okay," Clara said. But her voice shook.

Madame probed Clara's injury. It wasn't her whole right arm that hurt now, just a couple of fingers and her wrist where she had tried to break her fall. Clara cradled her arm against her body and the throbbing lessened.

"I'll help her," Holly volunteered.

Madame nodded. "Thank you, Holly. You may both be excused."

Clara put her good arm around her friend. Hot tears slipped down her cheeks and the other dancers stared as the pair made their way past them toward the dressing room.

"Same scene. From the top, please." Behind them, Madame rapped the tempo on the floor.

As if the rapping were an alarm, Clara woke up from her stunned state. The consequences began to dawn.

Holly opened the door for Clara, then climbed behind the wheel of the Triumph convertible and swerved out of the lot. Clara wasn't worried about her handling the manual gears on the Maestra's car, but she *was* worried about the speed. A ticket, and Holly had a few, would just top off her day.

"They're gonna kill me," Clara said, a fat drop of rain hitting her in the face. The hinges were broken on the little roadster's folding canvas top.

"Yeah." Holly jammed the clutch and shifted smoothly through the gears. "They're gonna killya."

"If you don't kill me first."

"Just wanna get you home."

Clara looked at Holly. The occasional raindrop was becoming more regular and her hair was beginning to frizz. "You're *not* taking me home."

The Triumph slowed to the speed limit. "My house?"

"No." There would be no one home at Holly's—no lights on and a forgotten television blaring.

"You gotta tell'em sometime, Clara."

"Yeah." Clara looked at herself in the visor mirror. Her hair hung limp against her neck. Her face was pale, her lips chapped. "But not now."

On the other side of the door, Johann and Sebastian yelped. Bolts unclicked, and Tashi's eyes appeared behind the chain. Asking no questions, she drove Clara straight to the university hospital. On the way Clara told her the story. The whole story.

Thanks to Tashi's presence and Clara's special ID, the hospital treated her and took x-rays.

"A sprain," the doctor pronounced, wrapping her right

wrist and fourth and fifth fingers in a splint. "Dance when you feel up to it. I don't think your schoolwork will be affected because you don't need your last two fingers to write. As for piano, I'd say not for a while."

Tashi pressed.

"Yes." The doctor patted Clara on the shoulder. "It is very possible you could play in the finals at the end of November. But you must give that wrist complete rest for at least two weeks. If you don't, you could risk a permanent weakness."

Clearly he didn't understand the implications of what he'd just said. Clara closed her eyes and ticked off the time that would be left to practice. Two weeks and two days. No one could win the Nicklaus with only two weeks and two days.

The steaming water had cooled to tepid by the time Clara stepped out of Tashi's tub. Tashi had been right about the bath. The hot water, or maybe it was the extra-strength aspirin, had calmed her. Or maybe it was the fact that when she called home, she had learned her parents were out to dinner. Clara told Danny she was with Tashi and was going to spend the night. When Clara was younger she had often spent entire weekends at Tashi's, so only the lack of planning would surprise them.

Being careful of the splint, Clara wrapped herself in Tashi's iridescent peacock-colored robe. The cuffs hit her mid-arm, the hem at the knees. Barefoot, she padded into the living room. The sofa was pulled out, the bed made up.

Clara stood at Tashi's piano and dragged the middle

finger of her left hand, her good hand, down the keyboard in a glissando. It hurt a little as the tender skin at the base of the nail hit the edge of each key. It was just how she felt, that going-down sound. Going down fast.

Tashi lit the flame of the gas heater in the fireplace. "You know, my darling, I still remember the day your parents brought you to me." She balanced a cup of tea on the doily of her armchair and settled into the feathers. At her feet, Johann and Sebastian curled on the ottoman like yin and yang. "You were—four?"

"Three," Clara corrected.

"I heard them coming, there was such a racket, so I peeked. They were holding you, each by one hand, swinging you between them down the hall." Tashi chuckled. "I tell you, my darling, those old halls never heard music as lovely as your laughter."

Clara was alert behind the swag of hair that hid her face. She tried to remember it—the grip of each big hand, the quiet hall—but it wasn't there.

"I bent down and shook your hand. 'My name is Natalia Petrovna Volkonskaya,' I said. 'But when I was a little girl just your size, my mother called me Natasha, and that's what you may call me, too.' You were very solemn. You shook my hand back . . ." Tashi paused, smiling at the memory. "And 'Natasha' came out 'Tashi,' of course.

"Then your mother told me, 'Yesterday, Clara climbed up on the bench and played'—and this last word your mother whispered, as if it was a secret—'Mozart.'"

"The Twinkle Twinkle Little Star theme," Clara put in.

Tashi nodded and went on with the telling. "'Note-perfect, two hands. The way my student had been trying to play it,' your father bragged. And your mother, she said, 'That was when we knew.'"

Clara looked up.

"'This child was born to bring music to the world.'"

"My mother said that?"

"I do not think you can imagine their excitement, my darling. Their eyes were starry. They felt chosen."

"And what did you think?"

Tashi humphed. "I was skeptical. But I had known your parents for many years, since before your father was on the tour. I thought, well, perhaps it is possible. After all, you had the genes." Tashi shrugged. "So I did the only thing I could do. I lifted you onto the bench."

"What did I play?"

"At first, nothing. You were more interested in the snow-globe. But we got around to the music. You played the Mozart, and a tune I didn't know. The theme song from 'Sesame Street,' your parents said. That afternoon I went to the faculty lounge and watched the show on television. I had to know, you see, what this music was that had captured you."

"And, when I played, what did you think?"

Tashi sipped her tea, then looked up at Clara. If her glasses hadn't already been dangling, she would have dangled them. "*Odin,* it was a huge talent."

Clara knew the numbers because Tashi sometimes lapsed into Russian when she counted beats.

"*Dva*—and this was just as important—you seemed to be having a very good time."

"And *tri?*" Clara asked.

Tashi shrugged, and hearing that she had slipped into Russian, answered in English. "And three, we began."

Clara fingered the little Russian folk tune on the piano, adapting it to her left hand. *And three, we began.* As simple as that. As complicated as that.

Tashi was quiet while Clara played.

"You must put away your worries about your hand, my darling," she said when the song was over. "It is quite possible you could still be ready for the finals. This injury may even help us. We shall see."

Clara rolled her eyes. It was a lighthearted "no way, Tashi, you're crazy" signal that she knew Tashi would understand.

"In the meantime, you are instructed to follow your doctor's orders—and mine. School, yes. Dance, yes. Yes to whatever it is girls your age ordinarily do." Tashi winked. "But no piano, no practicing, no Nicklaus. For now."

Forever, Clara thought. Tashi was in major denial. The competition was only every other year, so Clara wouldn't have another chance until she was nineteen. "I'm sorry I wrecked your chances for another winner," she said.

In earlier years, two of Tashi's students, both of whom were now touring artists, had won the Nicklaus. Serious competitors sought her out.

Tashi humphed. "Do not underestimate yourself, my darling. And I have better things to worry about than counting medals."

"But still—"

"But still nothing. Do me a favor and give it a rest."

Clara smiled at the slang.

"Besides," Tashi said, winking gently, "you know I have another chance for a winner."

"What?" Clara leaned toward her, as if to hear it again.

"Clara." Tashi tipped forward in the armchair with alarm on her face. "Surely you know?"

Know what? She knew of other students Tashi had entered, but none of them had made it past the Second Cut. Clara shook her head.

"Darling, I'm sure I mentioned a new candidate, coming to study with me, months and months ago . . ."

Clara would be the first to admit it was possible. She would have paid no particular attention to a new name, one more competitor. She shrugged. "I don't know."

Sounding embarrassed at the oversight, or possible oversight, Tashi rushed to explain. "Well, I suppose it is conceivable you didn't realize . . . You see, for purposes of the competition, I am not listed as the teacher. As a professional courtesy, I deferred, of course, to his longstanding instructor."

His. Tashi had said "his." Of the five finalists, three were male . . .

Tashi sat back in her chair. "I don't imagine you have heard him play, Clara. But he really is quite good."

Clara could feel her face whitening. Afraid she was revealing more than surprise, she cast her eyes down at the keyboard and cut Tashi off. "Tashi. Stop explaining and just tell me. What's his name?"

"Marshall Lawrence. Of course."

The keys seemed to shift.

After what felt like a long time but probably was not, Clara found her voice. "Marshall Lawrence. We met. I think. I mean, we did. During the Second Cut." She looked up and tried to make her voice normal. "Is he a university student?"

Tashi shook her head, and Clara saw that she was observing her carefully. "No," Tashi answered, stretching the word out.

So he was a private pupil, like Clara. "I'd like to hear him play."

"Don't worry, you will." Tashi chuckled. "As I said, he is quite good, Clara. You might be frightened by the competition." Clara expected her to wink, but she didn't.

Tashi read two chapters of her murder mystery out loud while Clara petted Johann and Sebastian. Then Tashi put a fragile yellowed telegram gently between the pages. "It reminds me of my place," she always said.

Reaching up, she turned off the lamp. With her hands on Clara's shoulders, Tashi guided her to the makeshift bed, then sat down beside her and pulled a silver brush from her pocket. Yet another of very few keepsakes . . .

Clara hadn't realized how sleepy she was until Tashi started to brush. Images floated in front of her half-closed eyes. The bookmark . . . The silver brush . . .

"Tashi," she asked, "where did the snow-globe come from?"

Her eyes opened in surprise; she hadn't meant to ask the question. The little she knew about Tashi's past she knew from her parents. There were other times she had wanted to ask, but Tashi usually avoided talking about Russia.

Tashi stopped brushing. "Clara, my darling. Such questions." Her voice sounded tired.

"I'm sorry. Forget I asked."

"No, no, hush." Tashi went back to brushing. "It is late. I will tell you, but not tonight. There's been enough talk for one night."

Tashi pulled the sheets back and Clara climbed in, arranging her splinted arm against her body.

God, she was beat. Tashi was right. Enough for one night. Way more than enough.

Tashi kissed Clara on the forehead, lifted a Pomeranian in each arm, and tiptoed out of the room.

Tashi's kid gloves gripped the giant steering wheel of the vintage Cadillac at ten and two, and she sat on an inch of *Clavier* magazines to see over the arc. She hadn't learned to drive until she was in her fifties, which was, she admitted, too late.

As they crept along the side streets, Clara's stomach churned. Tashi had fried potato pancakes and set out applesauce and sour cream, and Clara had felt obliged to eat.

Clara reached over to crank the window down but stopped, because she remembered: Tashi liked the windows up—the wind blew her hair. Untucking her T-shirt from the bib of her overalls, she dabbed at her face—using her splinted hand—then dropped her head back on the seat and concentrated on calming her stomach. If Tashi didn't hurry, wind-blown hair was going to be the least of the mess.

The driveway was too narrow for the Cadillac, so Clara said good-bye at the curb. Heading up the front walk, she draped her jacket off one shoulder, letting the splint show.

"That's it and I'm sorry."

Clara sat in a director's chair, elbows propped on the threadbare knees, her splinted right hand nested in her left.

She had told it straight. Already her stomach felt better.

Three times in the last hour, Clara's mother had stood up, left the room, shut doors, opened doors, returned, sat down, and made Clara repeat what she had missed. Clara's father had sucked in his salt-and-pepper beard and rubbed his palms on his pants. But now they sat still, on the edge of their bed in the corner of the den.

At last her father began. "You made a mistake."

Clara nodded.

The Maestra launched into her lecture. "Yes, you made a mistake, and it's a terrible one. And the dancing's not the worst of it. Or even the disobedience. But the lying, the sneaking out, night after night—Clara, how could you?"

Clara didn't answer.

The silence was ear-splitting. Finally, in an attempt to fill it, Clara began to count, slowly, in her head. She was up to 80 before her mother spoke again.

"I'll make some calls." Her mother reached across the bed for her briefcase, pulled out her day-planner, and flipped through phone numbers. "Find out which orthopedists are recommended. We need a second opinion. Maybe even a third."

"Mom, I really don't think—"

"Your hands are your life, Clara," her mother cut in. "We certainly are not going to take any chances." She turned to her calendar and counted. "If necessary we can take you out of school. There will be just enough time if you push yourself, but—"

"But we are not making that decision today," her father

interrupted, which he seldom did. "That decision depends on the wrist, the fingers, the doctors."

"I really think I can play, dad. I've been using my hand all morning—it doesn't even hurt."

"Clara, please," her father went on. "Let's not think about playing right now. Just rest and heal. Don't touch a key. It will be hard, I know . . ."

More silence.

Her mother paged through her day-planner. Her father stroked his beard.

"Mom, Dad. I know this isn't the best time to ask this." Her voice was level. "But there is one more thing we have to talk about."

Both parents looked squarely at her. Maybe it was the tone in her voice. They were used to arguing and manipulating, not plain speaking.

"I would like to stay in the Nutcracker."

Clara's mother crossed her arms. She opened her mouth, then shut it.

"It's important to me. And instead of storming off when I first brought it up, I should have kept talking—made the two of you realize how important." She looked from one to the other. "It will help fill the time until I can practice again. And I already asked the doctor. He said it wasn't a problem."

Clara's mother uncrossed her arms. "Truthfully, Clara," she said, sighing, "I think all the secrets have taken a bigger toll on your concentration than going ahead and dancing ever would have."

Her mother's voice sounded different, too. There was no trace of that maddening reasonableness Clara so often heard from the Maestra.

"If we take you out of the ballet now, you will only go on being distracted by what you think you are missing." Her mother looked at her father. "And, I admit, you were handling the schedule."

Clara's father gave his wife a nod.

"You be the judge, Clara," her mother said, picking her day-planner back up. "If you think you can handle things, go ahead and dance."

Clara's instinct was to jump up and hug her, but she didn't. Instead, she exhaled a "Thank you" and hoped her mother heard—probably not, though, because she was already on her way to the phone.

"You're welcome," her dad said gently, then stood up and left.

Clara relaxed in her chair. The muscles in her neck and shoulders loosened. If Danny had made his usual Saturday morning breakfast, there would be cold biscuit sandwiches for lunch. Clara popped up out of her chair and jogged toward the kitchen.

Second Movement

Two weeks later, on a Friday afternoon in mid-November, Clara sat—legs swinging—on top of her dad's desk, watching Lincoln High School's mixed chorus rehearse its Christmas program. She was still in the splint. Doctors two and three had concurred with number one—rest, wait, and see. With hours of extra time to fill, Clara had taken to staying late after school and riding home with her father.

Wearing a flowered shirt and wraparound sunglasses, Vince Lorenzo perched on his stool, head bobbing. From the risers, another forty-two pairs of sunglasses bobbed back at him.

"Day-O." The sing-song chant of boatmen loading bananas floated out over the room . . .

Clara grinned. What would the mall manager who had scheduled these kids for the holidays think when they showed up in their shades and cutoffs singing Caribbean folk songs? They'd be squeezed in between some other schools' "Silver Bells" and "Hanukkah, O Hanukkah."

Her dad jumped off his stool to add hips and turns. Clara let her torso sway and pulled up her legs to drum her knees—

Oops, the skirt. She had been dressing up more lately, but sometimes she still forgot about her sprawling limbs.

Across the room, voices rose and fell like ocean breezes. The nightworkers sang of daylight's approach . . . of the tallyman's coming . . . of quitting work and going home . . .

Clara eyed her chemistry book. She picked it up and dropped it into her lap. It was heavy. She didn't open it. Instead of her knees, she drummed the cover.

Those island rhythms. They sounded just the way Friday afternoon ought to sound . . .

The fact that it was Friday meant tomorrow was her follow-up appointment at the university hospital. As she drummed, she wiggled her fingers. She was sure the doctor would say she could practice again; she could feel the strength back in her hand. After her appointment, she was scheduled to meet Tashi in her office.

But following Tashi's instructions, Clara hadn't let herself think about any of that during the past two weeks. A boy in her chem class had asked her to be his study partner, and she had agreed. Twice she had gone to the movies with Holly and her friends. And tonight, after picking her mother up from orchestra rehearsal, Clara was going to a football game—the first of her life.

"Day-O." In front of Clara, the voices mounted. Perhaps light had truly arrived on the island and the workers would finally get their rest . . .

Clara's father—still dancing as he directed—looked over at her and stretched out his arm. "Come on, Clara. Dance with me."

Good grief. Everyone was looking at her, rattling their rainsticks in encouragement.

Clara dumped the chem book, hopped off the desk, and took his hand.

Backstage with her father and Danny, Clara studied Ellen Alexander between the necks of the string basses as the thundering final measures of the Brahms First Symphony crashed over the empty red seats.

Her mother's face dissolved into calm; she folded her hands on the stand. Fanned in front of the podium, the orchestra waited for its cue. The Maestra rested her baton along the top of her open score. "Thank you, everyone." She ran her fingers through the wet fringe of her short hair, then patted her face dry with a towel draped around her neck. Her features loosened into a broad smile. "Next rehearsal we will begin at letter G."

Eighty-seven musicians reached for their music and the shuffle began. No one would hear over the noise, but Clara shifted her satchel to her shoulder and slowly applauded.

A sea of feathered hats pitched left and right, and the brass blared out "The Talons of Lincoln's Eagles," only slightly out of tune. Greg Johnson, the boy who had asked Clara to be his study partner, jogged up the steps, bringing hot chocolate. He'd been sitting with Clara all second half, helping her follow the game.

Clara turned up the collar on her fringed suede jacket and accepted the drink. Wrapping her hands—as well as she could considering the splint—around the cup, she let the steam bathe her face.

Did accepting the hot chocolate make this a date? Was there any other seventeen-year-old girl in this stadium who had never been on a date? Or who didn't know for sure if she was on one?

She couldn't help smiling. Greg must have thought the smile was for him, because he slid closer and put his arm around her. Clara kept her face intact.

From twenty rows down, Holly flashed a thumbs-up, then went back to her cheers. Clouds puffed out of her mouth and her cheeks flushed to the color of her hair. Soon she had everyone—including Greg and Clara—back on their feet, where she had kept them most of fourth quarter.

On the field, the huddle broke, and a hush fell over the stadium. Lincoln was down by seven points and there were only seconds left.

Clara stashed her cup under her seat and clasped her hands together. In her ear, Greg ran the play-by-play.

The center snapped the football. The Lincoln quarterback, armed cocked, faded, farther and farther, then hurled a thirty-yard pass. Clara's head turned with the crowd's. In the end zone, the receiver bobbled the ball but held on to it.

A roar went up. Noisemakers twirled and horns honked and the band started in, yet again, on the out-of-tune fight song. Clara jumped up and down and clapped. Man, was this what ordinary life would be like? If she didn't play?

Clara froze. Around her, the crowd was going crazy, but she didn't breathe.

If she didn't play. God, what an if.

Kids were chanting, fingers in the air, "Two! Two! Two!"

She was born to play. She had been showered with gifts just so that she could. It was who she was, what she did.

Her eyes scanned the crowd. If she didn't play, she would be just like everyone else. If she didn't play, there would be no Nicklaus to prepare for. If she didn't play, this was how she would live, always . . .

Time out.

Clara inhaled deeply and began to breathe again.

Greg explained the team's options. The cheerleaders ran back on the grass and the crowd chanted along. "Lincoln's eagles, birds of prey . . ."

Clara pinned her eyes on Holly. She landed a string of flip-flops with a bounce that made the Oklahoma clay look like a springboard. Other images began to tumble in Clara's head: her dad, acting squirrely in the sunglasses; her mother, the prizefighter's towel draped; Holly, too, cheering herself on with no parent ever in the stands to see her. They were all just doing what they did, and they were having fun doing it.

The teams ran back onto the field. The referee blew his whistle, and the clock started its countdown.

The last two weeks had been fun for Clara. But the last two weeks weren't supposed to have been fun. They were supposed to have been hard. Clara swayed on her feet.

There was a snap, a fake, Lincoln was going for two. The crowd rose up on its toes . . . people stepped onto the bleachers . . .

Clara sat down.

The stadium exploded with whistles and sirens and noisemakers. The game horn sounded and kids hugged and danced and pumped their fists in the air.

Clara looked up from the bottom of a deep well, cheering fans on their feet all around her. When was the last time piano had made her feel like cheering?

Jammed together with half of Lincoln High School, Clara and Holly fought to keep their place in a crush of bodies that in no way resembled a line, while Greg and Holly's boyfriend-of-the-week held a table. The two girls faced each other, Clara ahead with her back to the counter.

Holly pulled her hair forward and sniffed. "McDonald's French-fry grease, layered over raspberry shampoo."

"Nice," Clara answered, wishing the line would move and that she had never agreed to come here.

Holly counted on her green and white fingernails, tabulating the orders she was supposed to bring back. "One Mac, two double CBs hold the pickle. It would be cheaper to get two number-two combination meals and super-size the fries and large the drinks, if you can even large the drinks on a combination, but—"

A group cleared out ahead of them and Holly nudged Clara backwards into the space. "You go first," she said, "I'm still doin' my calculus." She spun Clara around by the fringe of her jacket.

Marshall Hammonds Lawrence was behind the cash register.

Clara felt the blood drain from her face.

A pink flush crept into his.

God. She had wanted his next sight of her to be on-stage, at the piano. And here they were at McDonald's.

Clara brought her right hand out of her pocket for a half-wave. "Hi."

The flush faded and he squared his shoulders. "Gosh. It's always a surprise with you, isn't it?" He smiled. Under the fluorescence his eyes were even greener than she remembered. His gaze moved down her arm and he leaned over the counter. "Are you hurt?"

Clara held the splint up.

"Can you play?"

"I think so." She shrugged. "We'll know for sure tomorrow." She put her hand back in her pocket and changed the subject. "So you work here? I mean, obviously, I guess."

He nodded. "Usually my shift's during the week. But lately I've been trading my schedule around, to make room for extra lesson time."

Extra lesson time? Tashi didn't have any extra lesson time. Unless it was Clara's Monday-Thursday slot, which she hadn't been using for the past two weeks—

"Hey, buddy!" somebody yelled from behind them. "This is supposed to be *fast* food!"

The complainer must have pushed, because Clara lurched forward, the last domino.

"Guess I better take your order," Marshall said to her.

"Sure. Only I think I forgot it."

Holly cut in, an amused expression on her face. While she rattled off her order and offered the precise amount, calculated with tax, to the penny, Clara unbuttoned her jacket and reached for her money.

Did he notice the dress? The thin leather strap, angling between her breasts toward the coin purse on her hip? Was it normal to wonder such things?

Clara's turn came again. "Garden salad. Small fries. Medium diet."

He filled the order. She offered bills. When he dropped the change into her hand, his fingers brushed her palm.

"Thanks." She picked up the tray. "Guess I'll see you."

"Yes," he said, a little too quickly. "I want to. Clara."

Her shoulders were already turned, but when he said it, she stopped. She had never told him her name. Of course he would know the names of all the finalists, but somehow he would have had to match up the faces. She turned back. "How did you know my name?"

He hesitated, and the pink crept back into his cheeks. "Your nocturne book."

She nodded, then smiled.

He smiled back, then turned to the next customer. "Sorry for the wait, I'll throw in the drinks."

Clara made her way through the bodies. Here was another reason to play in the Nicklaus. Not that it was a very good reason. Not that she was seriously thinking of not playing. But if she didn't, she wouldn't see him again. Even more important, he wouldn't see her, wouldn't hear her.

God—she shuddered, nearly upsetting the drink on her tray—she couldn't believe she was thinking this way.

Clara volunteered to pick Danny up from basketball practice before her doctor's appointment. The squeak of Nikes on polyurethane met her at the door to the gym.

Sweating girls and boys were everywhere, passing balls between their legs and spinning them on their fingers.

She spotted Danny at the free-throw line, eyebrows raised. But if what the other kids were doing was any standard, he was taking too much time, too many bounces.

He took the shot. The ball hit the rim and bounced off.

Whistles chirped and all but a few kids tossed their balls into the bins. Danny went back around, dribbling his.

"You can do it, Danny," Clara yelled and crossed her fingers. "Keep your eye on the basket."

Several faces looked over at her, grinning. One face was Danny's, but he wasn't grinning. He flung the ball, sidearm, at the backboard. Without watching to see where it went, he spun on his heel and marched up to her. "Man, Clara, you are so embarrassing."

"Good grief, Danny, what'd I do? I thought I was being the supportive older sibling."

"You were being the meathead older sibling." He

grabbed his gym bag, shook out sweatpants, and pulled them on—inside out.

"Oh, come on, Danny." She put her arm around him, but he jerked free.

Clara stepped back. What was that all about? More than free throws. "I'm sorry. I don't know about this stuff—"

"No kidding."

"But just because you had one bad throw, don't take it out on me."

"It doesn't matter anyway." He headed for the door. "I'm quitting."

"What?" Clara chased after him.

"You heard." He strode down the narrow hall.

"Danny!" She ran to catch up. "This isn't some instrument you can just all of a sudden stop practicing. Basketball is a team sport."

"I thought you didn't know about this stuff, Clara." He kept his eyes straight ahead, walking in front of her.

"Well, it *is* a team sport, isn't it?"

He kept walking.

"Oh, come on, it was a joke." She poked him in the back of his rib cage.

He walked faster.

"Danny, you are so lucky to get to do all this fun stuff and you don't even know it."

He stopped short and she ran into him.

Turning, he faced her, blocking the hall so that everyone else who was coming or going had to stop too. "Clara, I know I call you a meathead lots. But I never realized. You actually *are* one." He walked away again.

Clara's mouth fell open. She was used to him calling her names, but this was different. He wasn't yelling.

"Danny, wait up." People turned their heads to listen. "You know what I'm saying—"

"Shut up, Clara."

"Karate, golf, string bass." She spoke over his shoulder. "Mom and Dad let you try anything you—"

"Shut up."

"—want."

They walked on in silence. When they reached the lobby, Clara hooked her hand into the strap dangling from his bag and pulled him toward the snack bar. He dropped the bag off his shoulder so that she was left holding it, facing him.

"Danny, I don't want to fight. I really don't." She looked at him. "Do you think we could just start over?"

He stood silent, arms crossed.

"Here. I'll buy you a drink." Before Danny could protest, she turned to the man behind the counter and ordered. "One large Dr. Pepper, one medium diet anything."

The cashier felt his way to the cups, ice, and buttons. Danny walked up beside her. He put his elbows on the counter and clasped his hands behind his neck. When he spoke, his voice was calm. "You really don't get it, do you?"

"Don't get what?" She slid the Dr. Pepper in front of him.

The cashier felt each coin before putting them into Clara's palm.

"Don't get what it's like to be the ungifted one."

The cashier spilled the coins on the counter.

"God, Danny! Mom and Dad don't label you like that."

"Think about it, Clara." Danny put the drink on the counter and left through the glass doors to the parking lot.

By the time Clara had gathered the coins and cups and caught up to him, his pace had slowed. Juggling both drinks, and with his gym bag on her shoulder, she walked beside him.

He kept his eyes on the pavement. "Why do you think I'm always changing instruments and sports and stuff, Clara?"

She'd had her theories: he was a goof-off; he was spoiled. She kept quiet.

"Name something, Clara. Anything that I'm really good at."

Danny made good grades. He had lots of friends. But they were bad answers. It would be better to name one single outstanding thing.

"Danny, please take this," she said, handing him the Dr. Pepper. "My hand is freezing."

He accepted the cup but didn't take a drink. Their feet hit the pavement in unison.

"Clara, use your meathead brain for one second and think. Here's me, stuck in this family of big shots—"

"That's crazy, Danny. No one's—"

"Man, Clara, just shut up and listen for once!"

She pressed her lips together.

"A dad who used to be an opera star. Before he gave it all up for you—"

"Daniel Vincent Lorenzo! Dad would die if he heard you

say that. Not to mention it's not true. I was only a baby when Dad decided to teach! He hated traveling. And anyway, if he did do it for me, he did it just as much for you."

"It was five years before I was even born, Clara."

She cleared her throat but didn't say anything.

"And this famous mother who gets interviewed on the *Today* show—who turns down jobs all over the place—"

"They decided not to move until we're both out of school. It was a family decision. Not because of me."

"Why do you think she even came here, Clara? Oklahoma City, Oklahoma"—he said it with a cowboy drawl—"the center of the universe for the performing arts."

"It was a good job for a young conductor. A nice place to raise a family." But she knew it sounded lame.

"You're the reason. They wanted you with Tashi."

Some truth there. But it was a factor, not the whole reason.

"And then I have this meathead sister—correction, *genius* meathead sister—who's gonna be a gazillion times bigger big shot than either one of them."

God, he had this all thought out.

He stopped walking and Clara stopped with him.

"And then there's me." He thumped his head. "Danny." He quoted their mother: "'Just a nice name we picked out of the baby-name book, sweetheart.'"

Clara was named after Clara Schumann, a nineteenth-century pianist, the first to perform entire concerts from memory and the wife of the composer Robert Schumann.

"And it's perfect, too. For a kid who can't play 'Mary Had a Little Lamb.'"

Clara remembered the violin recital when Danny was six. The notes had not been recognizable. Her family had covered their smiles with their programs.

"Danny," Clara said gently, "the violin's a very difficult instrument. You can't expect to pick it up in one year."

"Right, Clara, like you didn't pick it up in one year."

"I didn't." But in her one year of lessons, she had studied through Book Four. "Not very well."

Danny kicked the sidewalk, then looked away, talking to the horizon. "Stupid, stupid, stupid. Two weeks—my sister's not practicing—they'll stop obsessing—I think—for once. All they did was obsess more."

Clara remembered the Maestra's most recent dinner conversation. *I hope you're not carrying books in that arm, sweetheart. Why don't you take my tape recorder to school, for notes.* Suddenly, Clara wished she could put her arms around her brother.

"I'm stuck, see—" He was still talking to the horizon. "With this sister, see—" There was a rising quaver in his voice. "This huge . . . *thing* . . . hanging around in my life, in my house, with my mom and my dad. And she has the nerve to tell me how lucky I am?" He swiped the sweaty blond bangs out of his eyes, then turned to face her.

"They love you, Danny."

"I know." He took three steps, stopped at a trash can, and dropped the full cup into the empty bin. "But they love you more."

The cold blunt side of the blade traced a line up her forearm as the assistant cut away the soft-wrap under the splint. He peeled the fabric back to reveal Clara's wrist. Her mother and father leaned in to see.

Clara held her right arm up to her left. Next to the healthy limb, the injured one looked shrunken and pale. Her father's brows furrowed and her mother's teeth pressed dents into her lower lip.

There was a rustle of charts and the doctor entered, x-rays in hand. "So how's our young Van Cliburn?"

Clara struggled to put confidence into her eyes and voice. Her parents would be scared to death if they saw or heard anything less. "Fine, just fine."

"Her arm is so thin," her mother put in.

"Perfectly normal after weeks in a splint," the doctor said, holding the x-rays up to the light. "Muscles atrophy quickly, but they come back just as fast."

The slightest look of relief passed between her parents.

The doctor took her hand and began moving the fingers, one by one. Then her wrist, turning it over, cocking it from side to side. The fingers didn't hurt, but the wrist did. Clara winced but she kept it to herself, only blinking with each shot of pain.

"Any discomfort?"

She shook her head.

She remembered last night's football game, her thoughts of not playing in the Nicklaus. God, those really had been wild imaginings. Because here, with her parents—she looked from one to the other—she knew with certainty. Not playing was impossible.

"Then I'd say you're as good as new." He patted her

shoulder and addressed her parents. "If there had been pain, it might have meant a hairline fracture we weren't picking up on the pictures. I suspected something like that when she first came in, but I didn't want to worry anyone unnecessarily. Lucky for you folks, I guess I was wrong. First time for everything." He chuckled as he tossed the used splint into the can.

Clara looked up. "What if there had been a fracture?"

He slipped the x-rays back into the envelope. "I would have had to keep you immobilized a few more weeks."

"Should she take any special care of it, do you think?" her father asked. "Work up slowly with her practice time?"

"Just do what feels comfortable. If it hurts, rest. Pain is the body's way of telling us to stop."

Her mother picked up her father's hand and squeezed it.

"And now, Miss Piano Star," the doctor said as he marked the charts, "I understand from my conversations with your mother that after you win this contest, you're going to Juilliard for four years."

Clara eyed her mother. She didn't know there had been conversations.

"I have just one favor to ask for healing you in the nick of time."

"Sir?"

He saluted, touching the corner of the chart to his forehead. "Tickets to your first concert in Carnegie Hall."

Clara traded looks with her parents—anyone could rent

Carnegie Hall—and tried to smile as the doctor backed out the door. "Sure. I guess."

With her shoes off and her legs curled under her, Clara sat sideways on the couch beneath the window in Tashi's office. She had spent a lot of time here, listening to tapes and CDs and old recordings, comparing other artists' interpretations of the music she studied. It was her spot, and she especially loved it in the late fall and early winter when the sun came in from the south.

Tashi sat angled toward her in the matching tufted armchair, legs crossed at the ankles and gold lamé slippers on her feet. On the tea table, the Beethoven score lay open.

"Before you play this concerto, my darling," Tashi said, pouring more tea, "I wish to tell you something."

Clara sipped and lifted her eyes.

"I kept you from playing this music for so long because I thought perhaps . . . if you didn't play the concerto, if you were *forbidden* to play it—" She paused, aligning her cup in the groove. "You might find you needed to play it."

She set the saucer on the table. "And then this business with your wrist came along." She sighed, chest bouncing. "I thought, God is helping me. Two more weeks, she will die to play it. Perhaps."

Clara balanced her own cup and saucer on the window sill and looked out through the wavy glass. Below her, university students lounged on the steps of the music building.

"And now here we are. Beginning. And what I want you

to know is . . ."

Clara kept her eyes on the students in the quad, but in her peripheral vision she could see Tashi's glasses swinging.

"Just because the doctor says you can play, it doesn't mean you should."

Clara held still. Did the circles under her eyes give away her restless night?

"Clara, are you sure?"

"Sure of what? My arm?"

"You tell me."

"My arm is fine. Stop worrying."

There was a long pause.

"Clara, my darling, you should not play this concerto until—unless—you yearn to play it. Look me in the eyes and tell me."

On the other side of the window, a student took his skateboard out of his backpack and glided down the sidewalk. Not until he had disappeared around the corner of the music building did Clara finally turn her eyes.

Tashi asked again. "The Beethoven Concerto for Piano and Orchestra in C Major. Do you yearn to play it?"

There was too much at stake to consider any other answer. "Yes."

Somehow five hours went by. They spent the whole time on the first movement, experimenting with dynamics. Her fingers felt clunky—not just the hurt ones, all of them—and her wrist was a little sore. And she was starving. The thought of going to McDonald's crossed her mind.

"Enough for one day, my darling." Tashi closed the concerto, so frayed the strings showed through the binding. "Especially enough for that arm." Tashi kissed her own palm and pressed it against Clara's cheek, then pulled herself up from the chair and went into her office.

Clara stood and stretched, then hunted for keys in her satchel. She could hear the click as Tashi turned on the hot plate to make more tea.

"Listen, darling," Tashi called out. "I was wondering, about your next lesson—"

Opening the door to the hall, Clara nearly fell over the front wheel of a rusted Schwinn bicycle that came rolling through. "My gosh, Marshall." She hadn't meant to call him by name, it had just popped out.

He nodded and walked the bike in.

"Marshall, Marshall." Tashi padded in, teacup rattling. "I'm so glad you're here. You know Clara, I believe?"

Marshall parked his bike against the wall and turned around smiling. "We've met."

He must go everywhere by bike. Probably he didn't have a car, and the McDonald's was close. Maybe he lived in one of the garage apartments scattered around the campus. She knew most of them—it was her neighborhood too—and wondered which one.

"Before you go, Clara darling, I was wondering if you might be willing to share your next lesson?" Tashi turned to Marshall. "You will understand, I'm sure. Clara needs her lesson times back, now that her hand is healed."

"Of course."

"However, on this Monday, I thought perhaps you could both come. I have a rare Rubinstein recording of the concerto that I would like the two of you to hear. It would save time to listen together. Clara, do you think this would be helpful?"

"Sure, Tashi, I sink zis vould be helpful."

Tashi winked. Clara was the only one she would let get away with that.

Marshall began to pull music from his backpack, and Clara put her hand on the knob again.

"And Clara." Tashi's voice stopped her. "Sometime I want the two of you to get together and play—critique each other's work. The time is too tight to do it during lessons, but I thought perhaps—" She looked back and forth. "The two of you, you could arrange this?"

Their eyes met. Clara was embarrassed because she knew Tashi saw.

"Uh, sure, Tashi, at least, I guess—" With her hand still on the knob, Clara searched Marshall's face for some sign of encouragement. He nodded and she nodded back. "We'll arrange it."

When her mom said she was ready, Clara walked out of the dressing room. Her dad was shifting restlessly on the too-small love seat, Danny was guzzling the free Coke. But when she crossed in front of them, they sat straight and still.

That Sunday afternoon, Clara's mother had come rushing in. She'd found the perfect dress for the New Year's concert. The store had a size eight, Clara's size. Now that her wrist had the okay, they should put it in layaway, not run the risk it might be gone before the holidays—if Clara liked it, of course, and she knew that she would. As they headed out the door, she had made Clara go back and put on her plungiest bra. Clara had groaned, but her mother had insisted. She wasn't going to all this trouble to have something tacky showing.

Their eyes had moved in unison, up and down the mannequin, as they stood together in front of the store windows. Black sequins completely covered the fitted top, made out of a stretchy material with tiny tucks. There was a V-neck front and back, and the sequins continued several inches past the waistline to the beginning curve of the hips. From there, three filmy layers of snow white silk floated to the floor.

"What about Tashi's no-sparkles rule?" Clara had whispered, still staring.

Her mother had waved her off. "Rules for contests are completely different from rules for performances. A guest artist is supposed to sparkle."

A guest artist. Her mother thought of Clara as a guest artist.

Clara had never been in a dressing room as fancy, with a settee and a glass of mint iced tea brought in on a tray. Unbuttoning her jeans, she had turned over the dangling tag. No way.

Still, she couldn't resist putting it on. Even without shoes and hose, even without fixing her hair, she had to admit . . .

Now, Clara stood in front of her dad and Danny. Her father's eyes were glued.

"Well. Somebody say something."

At last her father spoke, "'Cindrillon' by Jules Massanet. Act two. The ball. Cinderella enters and everyone gasps, astonished by her beauty. Pandolfe, Cinderella's father, is in the crowd, but he doesn't recognize his daughter."

Clara's father stood, and was suddenly singing. *"'O la surprenante aventure! O la charmante créature! . . .'"*

Danny rolled his eyes in the direction of the clerk, a sign to indicate they were the only sane ones there. But the clerk seemed to be enjoying the opera, or was doing a good job pretending to.

Clara's mom guided her to the three-way mirror. "It's perfect." She checked the hooks and eyes. "The black is sophisticated. But the white keeps it young enough for seventeen, a debut. No sleeves. The torso will move, and the skirt falls just right." She watched while Clara walked and sat, bringing three different seats until they found one that was piano bench height.

Finally, the clerk was out of earshot. Clara spoke under her breath. "But Mom!"

"But Mom what?" She held the hair off Clara's neck.

"We can't afford this dress."

"Oh, don't worry about the money, sweetheart."

"What do you mean, don't worry about the money? We always worry about the money."

"I've got it all figured out." Clara's mother lowered her voice. "I have my Concert in the Park check. I was just hoping to find something this perfect to spend it on."

"No way, Mom, I'm not going to let you do that."

Ellen Alexander found her daughter's face in the three-way mirror. "Clara, indulge me in a moment of motherhood." Fixed on Clara from every direction, the eyes were a radiant blue. "I think about giving you this dress the way most mothers think about giving their daughters a bridal gown."

She turned Clara to the side and checked her profile. "All you have to do is take it, enjoy it, and have fun when you wear it."

"Hey." Holly sat down next to Clara in the front row of study hall. "Look what I got done in computer last hour." She opened her cheerleading bag to reveal an American Lit paper, neatly printed out and clipped.

Clara glanced at it, then went back to scribbling French verb conjugations with her gnawed-off pencil. "Sorry I didn't make Saturday," she said without looking up.

She had been invited to a party, but that was before she came home from the five-hour session at Tashi's, and before she decided she needed to spend Saturday night working on the second movement.

Holly dropped her voice. "Greg was there, saying how much he needed to study chemistry. Kept looking at the door."

"Well, he shouldn't have. It wasn't a definite thing. I'm back to practicing. Hard. Hardest I ever have in my life, since you asked."

"Sounds like fun."

"I get up, I practice, I go home, I practice, I go to bed, I practice in my head. Every now and then, just for laughs, I do something really rowdy like brush my teeth."

Holly pawed through her bag, then held up dangling bald eagle earrings from the Nature Store. "What about your Lit paper?" she asked, slipping the earrings in.

"If I turn it in the week after the competition, I'll lose only one letter grade."

"Clara Lorenzo, Lincoln High School Queen of Extra Credit, is gonna give up one whole letter? It'll sink your four point."

"It's not a four point."

"Excuse me. Your three point nine eight." Holly shook her head. "Anyway, what about Nutcracker rehearsals?"

"Madame's on the second act. She won't be calling my scenes for a while." For the first time since Holly sat down, Clara stopped writing and looked at her, eagles twirling beneath her lobes. "The thing is, Holly, the Nicklaus is the single most important thing I may ever do in my life." She went back to the verbs. "As a matter of fact, I want you to be there. You'll like it. There'll be reporters and cameras."

"Sounds as big as cheerleader tryouts."

"Very funny."

"Who's being funny?"

"Just don't plan on seeing much of me till after the twenty-eighth. Right now, papers and parties and school"—she motioned to the auditorium with the pencil stub—"even the Nutcracker. They're all a distraction."

"And your chemistry partner, is he just a distraction?"

"Just a distraction."

"And Ronald McDonald?"

Clara looked up at her. "Marshall is the competition. Marshall helps me keep my focus."

Holly's turquoise eyes were laughing and she cracked her gum. "Major distraction."

Clara curled in the corner of the couch. Marshall completely filled the other end, legs extended in front, shoulders leaned back, fingers laced over his abdomen, and eyes closed. Between the two of them was a careful space, occupied by the worn leather backpack.

The recording was from Tashi's personal collection, a scratchy old album. They would be expected to make intelligent commentary after, and usually, by now, Clara would have filled pages and pages with her crimped handwriting. But the spiral ring in her hand was blank.

It was toward the end of the slow second movement when Tashi—who had been taking her own notes at her desk on a pad of staff paper—stood up. Whispering that she needed to catch another professor before he left for the day, she stepped out.

Marshall didn't open his eyes. Had he heard Tashi leave? Was it possible he didn't know what to say or do, either?

The recording was thin and dotted with static, but Rubinstein managed to make the melodic second movement sound warm and full. Clara closed her eyes. The performance was timeless, coming to them through decades. The pianissimo was so soft, as soft as the worn leather backpack would be. She almost reached out and touched it.

The Largo ended and the needle retraced its final groove. Neither of them moved.

The critique of the Rubinstein ended promptly at six. Clara lingered beside Marshall as they walked down the hall. Usually she took the stairs, but he stopped at the elevator because of his bicycle and she went along. She punched "1." Marshall punched "B." The practice rooms were in the basement.

The elevator doors opened on the first floor. Clara said good-bye and stepped out. Behind her, the doors shut—then opened again.

She waited, eyes wide.

There was a trace of hurried shyness. Would she like to come down with him for a minute?

Forty-eight cubicles, ten feet by ten feet. Clara had spent time in all of them and she knew: except for the makes of the pianos, the rooms were identical—a keyboard facing the door so your back was to the window, a bench, a light. Her first choice was number 26, then 24, then 2. If they weren't open, she took whatever was handy.

He unlocked room 12, the last on that hall. She didn't know you could get keys, reserve rooms for keeps. Why hadn't Tashi told her?

Reaching around, he flicked the switch and let her go first.

She took in a breath. Against the wall, where it couldn't be seen through the narrow window, was a sleeping bag. Lined up on top were a shaving kit, a box of Tide, a travel iron, a can of spray starch, and plastic bags with socks and underwear folded inside. A stack of music served as an end-table for a CD player, earphones, and a tower of CDs.

"Marshall, is this for real?"

"As real as it gets," he said, squeezing his bicycle between the upright piano and the wall. Some of the rooms had grands, but she could see why he had chosen one that didn't.

He motioned toward the door. "Would you mind if I, you know, closed it? If anybody saw—"

"Sure. Of course." Clara turned and closed the door herself. She hung her music satchel over the knob and punched in the lock.

He had mounted a towel bar on the back of the door, and a few clothes hung on hangers. T-shirts, ironed. Jeans, folded. Three collared shirts like the one she had seen him wear at McDonald's. She realized it was like snooping in somebody's closet, and she turned back around. "Does Tashi know?"

"Oh, she knows." He laughed. "Dr. Volkonskaya is the one who bribed the custodian to leave the key in the door."

Picking up the lid of the piano bench, he pulled out a bag of Oreos, then motioned to the sleeping bag. "Would you like to sit down?"

Clara sat, cross-legged, at one end of the makeshift couch. Under her, the floor was hard and cold. Marshall sat at the other end and passed her an Oreo.

"Piano cookies," Clara said, taking one. "My brother used to call them that because they're black and white."

"One brother? That's it?"

She nodded. "How about you?"

"No brothers." He watched her. "Six sisters, though."

Clara choked on the cookie. "Six sisters?"

He grinned. "Six."

They ate the cookies in silence. When she was through, Clara brushed off her hands and wiped them on her jeans. "Okay. So tell me the story. How does a person end up living in a practice room?"

"There's not much story. My apartment manager raised the rent." He fiddled with the cellophane. It crinkled and popped. "It was a couple of days before the Second Cut. One night I was down here practicing, and when I went upstairs the sun was up."

He had practiced all night without knowing?

"It was an accident, but it gave me the idea. I mean, the rooms are open twenty-four hours a day, and I was already here whenever I wasn't at work. The more I thought about it, the more an apartment seemed like a waste."

"What about showers and laundry and stuff?"

"My ID from Dr. Volkonskaya gets me into the dorms."

"But with a job, and"—she tipped her eyes toward the bicycle—"no car, your expenses couldn't be that much."

"Yeah, but the decor works great with the starving-artist routine I use to pick up girls."

He waited for her to react, but she didn't.

"Smile, Clara." He leaned back against the wall. "Do you realize, I have only seen you smile one time."

McDonald's, when he admitted getting her name from her nocturne book. She changed the subject. "Do your parents know you're living here?"

"Clara. I'm twenty."

"Right. Well. Still, I'd think they'd want to help out."

"I'm sure they'd love to help out."

Too late, Clara realized her gaffe.

He folded the top of the cookie bag down. "My family's from Austin. My dad's a letter carrier, my mom manages a laundromat. My sisters are eighteen, sixteen, fourteen, twelve, ten, and six." He counted them on his fingers.

He had great hands. Big enough to easily play a tenth, and the skin was smooth and tight.

"I was a business major at the University of Texas. But instead of studying I'd practice. My grades dropped and I lost my scholarship."

"Oh."

"It was okay, really." He had creased the bag in accordion pleats now, and he folded and unfolded them. "Clara—when I used to try and think of myself in the future, you know, in business—well, I would just go blank."

He stopped folding the pleats and looked at her. "What I finally realized was, I could not imagine my life—I could not imagine any life at all—without piano at the center of it."

He went back to the pleats. "This is my third try at the Nicklaus—I guess I told you that . . ." He paused, then started again.

"Not to sound like I'm playing to violins in the background or anything, but when I was sixteen, my tape didn't make the First Cut. When I was eighteen, I rode the bus up, and missed the finals by two points. Twenty, this is it."

"How'd you end up with Tashi?"

"I sent Dr. Volkonskaya a tape. Told her that I'd been working on the concerto for a year—"

A whole year on a straightforward student competition piece?

"—and that I'd like to come study with her, but—and I was very specific about this—I wanted to come only if she thought I had a shot at winning."

So Tashi thought he had a shot. Clara looked away, then back.

"Anyway, to wind this epic up—" He reached over to the piano bench and tucked the crinkling cellophane away. "My sisters and I have a pact—big kids helping little kids till everybody's through school. Right now anything extra goes to my next-in-line sister. She's a freshman, pre-law."

He sounded proud of her. That was nice, for a brother to be proud of his sister. "Suppose you win the Nicklaus and go to New York? What happens to your sister then?"

"No matter where I am, there'll always be some other side job, for whichever sister, until I'm making a living from music. But the Nicklaus, well"—he gazed at the piano—"I try not to even let myself think about it. The best teachers, free, for four years . . ."

There were so many questions she wanted to ask, but his mention of sisters had reminded Clara of Danny and her parents. The picture of them sitting around the table with the Thursday enchilada casserole going cold tugged at her.

"Marshall, I don't want to, but I've got to go." She unfolded her legs and stood up.

"It's okay." He stood with her. "Anyway, I've got to practice. Not all of us were born prodigies—"

"Marshall, no, I wasn't a prodigy." She already had the door open, but she stopped and turned around. Probably he was only teasing—he would know prodigies practiced as much as anyone else—but still, she had to make this clear.

"Oh, I've done some checking," he said. "I know."

"No. You don't."

He looked surprised. "All right," he said cautiously. "If you say so. Not a prodigy. A virtuoso—"

She started to shake her head.

"Clara, I know. Your Mozart—authentic, natural. Your Prokofiev—diamonds. The Debussy, maybe a hair too much pedal but it didn't matter because you brought the melody out so clearly—"

"My program?" she whispered, stunned by the revelation.

"I—well . . ." Pink crept up his neck. "I found out what time you were up and went back."

She remembered Sunday afternoon of the Second Cut. The big stage, the auditorium, mostly empty except for the judges and a few scattered groups. "But," Clara stammered, "I looked—"

"You looked for me?"

She nodded, realizing what she was confessing.

"Did you look in the balcony?"

Why would she have, when there was hardly anyone there?

"So I *do* know, Clara. Your talent is . . . is . . ." He took a step toward her and his hand reached out. But whatever the instinct was, he didn't follow it, because his arm stopped in midair, then dropped stiffly to his side.

He looked down and his voice dropped too. "Clara, I—I imagine you—sometimes—the orchestra tapping their bows—your hair up—in a long dress—" He swallowed and the green eyes came tentatively back to her. "Red. You should wear red. It will be beautiful with your hair and eyes in front of the black and white—"

He looked back at his feet. "I'm sorry." He straightened his shoulders, but his arms were still stiff at his sides. "Am I embarrassing you? Or am I just embarrassing me."

"No. Neither."

His eyes dared to find hers. "What a life you have waiting for you." He sighed and seemed to relax a notch. "Playing with the finest orchestras, and recording, and traveling—" He was talking faster. "Living your music twenty-four hours a day—"

Suddenly, she couldn't breathe.

The panic must have shown on her face because he took a quick step back. The green eyes looked confused, maybe even hurt.

"Bye" was all she could get out. She grabbed her satchel off the knob and left the door swinging.

For the next ten days, she only practiced. As for school, the Maestra thought the wrist should rest at least part of the day, so Clara still went. But really, she didn't. Really, she sat at her desk and practiced the concerto, just without a piano.

She told Greg she couldn't be his study partner. In spite of Holly yammering that she needed a break, she didn't think of going to a football game. She washed her hair only every other morning, and she never took time to blow it dry. She dropped her regular ballet classes, and she cut her jogging back to the two-mile minimum.

Her mother doubled up in one car with her dad so that Clara could have the Triumph. Her parents even backed off dinner. She bought yogurt at the Stop-N-Go on her way from school to the music building, and dropped the cup, warm and half-eaten, in the trash when she left after midnight.

Once her dad said something about her lack of sleep, her not eating right. But she could tell they were trying hard to stay out of it, to let her work her own way.

Danny volunteered to take over her chores. She agreed but offered to do double duty after the competition. He hesitated, but Clara persisted, and at last he shrugged and said okay.

Marshall she avoided, although when she went to the basement she always walked by the narrow window for a glimpse of his back. She remembered studying his back that first time at the bulletin board, wondering how to get his attention. She remembered the way his shoulder blade moved under her hand. But she never knocked on the practice room door, nor did she expect him to come knocking on hers. One afternoon the room next to his had been free. She found another room, as far away as possible.

She didn't keep track of the hours she spent at the piano. There was no time to keep time. Her wrist was neither better nor worse. She ignored it.

She practiced every passage, even the little three-note turns, note by note with the metronome. Realizing the pendulum was merely mechanical, she asked her parents if they could afford a seventy-dollar digital one. Her mother came home with a new metronome that night.

She was obsessive about naming the notes and chords in her head. It was her insurance policy: if her fingers forgot, her brain would inform them as fast as the next sixty-fourth note. It was a terrifying lesson she had learned years ago, one that occasionally still gave her nightmares. At her seventh-grade recital, she had been playing a series of Bach inventions when suddenly she began to question every move of every finger: was it an A or a G or a C that came next? She stopped, mid-phrase, and skipped to the next invention. Afterward, Tashi had taken her shaking body in her arms. "So. We have that out of the way." Clara had buried her head in her teacher's neck. "Darling, everyone falls asleep at least once. Be glad your nap came early, and not at a time when it really mattered." Then Tashi sent her back to the piano to play the invention through.

This time, though, thanks to Clara's prior studies of the concerto and the silent weeks of reading the music with only a pencil, she knew the notes in a way she had never known any others. She felt she knew these notes as Beethoven must have known them.

She played the concerto in bits. When she had one phrase the way she wanted, she put the series of phrases together to make the overarching phrase. When she had the overarching phrases right, she put them together to make the section. When she had the sections right, she put them together to make the movement.

It was like beading a necklace—Clara's metaphor, not Tashi's—picking just the right stone to come next. The beads were separate but touching. Sometimes after a few beads, she found she didn't like the colors she had strung next to each other and then she had to take the last beads off and try again. At the end she held the necklace up and judged—not as the creator, but as the buyer.

With the finals only a week away, a plan was approved—by Clara, Tashi, and her parents, sitting around the kitchen table late one night. The competition was the following Monday. On the Wednesday evening before, Clara would go to the Nutcracker walk-through. Afterward, she would take a break, go out with Holly for a movie or pizza, nothing late, nothing rowdy.

Thursday would be Thanksgiving. Her parents and Danny

were driving to Dallas to be with her grandparents. They thought she could spare the time and wanted her to come with them, but she was looking forward to the day alone.

Clara would spend Friday with Tashi, who was going to accompany her, playing the orchestra's part on the second piano. Most competitions prohibited teachers from accompanying their own students, but the Nicklaus encouraged the practice because it was a scholarship and students were recommended by their teachers. That Friday would be Clara's and Tashi's last time to work together, because on Saturday Tashi would be working with Marshall.

By Sunday she would be ready. She would spend only a couple of hours at the piano, let her mind clear.

Excused from school, she would spend most of Monday waiting. The first of the five finalists was scheduled to begin at noon. Allowing for tempo differences, the concerto took about thirty-eight minutes to play, and each performer would start on the hour. The time in between was for the judges to finish their notes, confer, and take a break. They played in order of points, and Clara, as the leader, was last at four o'clock. Her father had a substitute for school; the Maestra had canceled orchestra rehearsals. Holly had permission to drive her dad's pickup and would bring Danny after school.

Although her parents and Tashi would sit through all five performances, Clara would not. She could be in the building and occasionally slip in and out of the auditorium, down to the practice rooms, or up to Tashi's office to make tea and rest. She told them, however, that she intended to hear her closest competitor's entire concerto. They weren't sure it was a good idea, but they didn't overrule her.

The final standings placed Clara ahead of Marshall by four points, and both of them ahead of the next contender by more than twenty. Barring a disaster, one of them would finish first and the other would finish second.

Clara's hand floated on the backstage barre, set up for the dancers to stay warm between scenes. She stretched to the floor in a low port de bras.

The Nutcracker walk-through was over, and everyone except the crew had left. Holly was in the dressing room, changing and probably completely redoing her makeup. Clara was just going to slip a coverup on over her leotard.

A stagehand had turned on a radio and Clara stretched to the tenor saxophone music. God, it felt good to move. Her body was stiff from the week of sitting at the piano. If she was going to be a concert pianist, she was going to have to schedule more exercise.

At her last lesson Tashi had told her she was clenching up, tightening her jaw. "Your energy is trapped in a whirlpool," Tashi said, massaging the back of Clara's neck while she played. "Sing 'da da da' with the melody. It will keep your jaw loose, keep the notes flowing like a gentle waterfall, down your arms and over your fingers." Tomorrow, Clara had to remember to "da da da" . . .

But no more thinking about piano. It was Wednesday night before Thanksgiving, her party night.

"Dancer on stage. Dancer on stage." The microphoned

voice came from nowhere and everywhere. "Quickly, please."

Should she go? "Dancer" probably meant soloist.

Clara crept onto the stage. Bits of colored tape marked blocking on the floor. Behind her, the back curtains were open, exposing the brick wall of the Civic Center. The red and blue footlights were on. Past them, Clara could see an outline in the violet mist. Someone seated in the center. Probably the stage manager—the source of the voice—with headphones and a mike.

"Thank you. Downstage right, please. And move. We're checking the shadows on your face and we need you to move."

Clara walked downstage right. What did the voice mean, move? Did the voice think she could just move? Just like that?

"Move, please," the tired voice came again. "You are a dancer, miss, and dancers move."

Self-consciously Clara began her Scene I minuet, but it didn't work with the bluesy jazz. She changed to an adage combination she remembered from class.

"Downstage left, please."

Clara stopped and walked downstage, gave up the adage, and improvised. Had anyone ever choreographed a ballet to a saxophone solo? It seemed to be working.

She was loosening up, feeling less shy. After all, what did it matter? There wasn't anyone to see her except a couple of stagehands.

Suddenly a blinding white light beamed down on her. So

this was what it was like to dance in a spotlight.

Her silhouette moved against the red brick. Her silhouette was dancing well. The guy backstage must be watching because he turned the radio up. God, it really did feel good to move.

Her body was so tired of not moving. She held a back extension longer and higher than she knew she could. This time when the voice told her to move stage left, she didn't stop and walk over, but melted out of the arabesque and danced there. Probably the only time she'd ever dance in a spotlight, might as well enjoy it . . .

"Okay, thank you, dancer. Kill the spot."

The beam disappeared. Clara slumped. The radio was still on, but it didn't sound the same without the spotlight.

Holly walked in from the wings. "Wow, Clara, I didn't know you could move like that."

As she said it, the stage manager strode past them in his headphones, hurrying to the next detail.

If he'd been up here, in the wings . . .

Clara looked again for the figure in mist. She asked Holly, "Who is that out there?"

"You mean you don't know? She's been here all rehearsal."

Clara squinted through the haze, and realized. It wasn't headphones the figure was wearing, but a hat with a feather. There was only one person in the world who dressed like that. "Tashi."

"Of course Tashi. I thought you invited her."

As they watched, the figure stood, worked her hand into

one glove, and draped her stole. Clara thought she would come to the stage, but she turned up the aisle and left through the back doors.

It was Thanksgiving Day and her family was in Dallas. The house was quiet except for the scratching of Clara's pencil as she wrote the numbers in over the tops of the notes. Writing fingering in helped implant it in her brain.

Tashi had worried it might be too late to be changing things, especially fingering, but when Clara tried the new fingerwork, she had instantly preferred the way it fit her hand. She had assured Tashi—she could reprogram her muscle memory on the little section in ten minutes.

The doorbell chimed. On Thanksgiving Day at three o'clock in the afternoon? Clara clicked off the piano light. And at the front? Everyone they knew came in through the kitchen. She stuck the tooth-marked pencil behind her ear and peeked through the hole. The worn leather backpack.

She yanked the pencil out, unclipped her hair, and shook her head. God, and she was barely decent, in the remnants of one of Danny's old sweatshirts. It was cropped at the waist, and the sleeves were cut out so that the black straps of her athletic bra showed through the big armholes. The bra was made to be seen, but still.

She stuffed the hair clip in her jeans pocket and opened

the door. "My gosh, Marshall."

Bike propped on his hip, he slipped the backpack off his shoulder and took out a shoebox tied with a string. "Care package from Dr. Volkonskaya," he said, offering it. "Turkey, et cetera. She thought your day might be 'a tad bleak,' as she put it, and sent me over. I'm staying with her till Monday."

"You got kicked out?"

"Let's just say my hotel closed for the holidays." He grinned. "Uh . . . may I come in?"

His fingers brushed hers as he put the box into her hands. She held the door while he parked his bike in a corner of the porch.

"And we're supposed to eat this?"

"I think that was her general idea." He stepped inside, eyes wandering over the music room. "I mean, it is Thanksgiving. But we're under strict instructions to work after we eat. I think she's pretending to be mad at us—you know, that we never, well, got together."

Clara had not forgotten telling Tashi that the two of them would arrange a critique session. But she hadn't ever felt bold enough to act on it. Maybe he hadn't either.

Marshall continued, "But she was very firm. I have to be back by dark. I'm not sure if she thinks I need to get back to practice, or if it's her version of chaperoning."

Clara waved toward the music room. "So what do you think?"

"It's a beautiful workspace."

With metal shelves and cut-out cereal boxes?

"The egg-and-dart moldings . . ."

Clara looked up. She had never thought much about the old-fashioned moldings that framed the ceiling.

"The polished wood floor. These instruments . . ." His eyes lingered on the curves of her mother's Yamaha, the carved legs of her father's rosewood.

"Would you like to play?" She held out her arm to take his backpack, and he handed it to her. It was as soft as she had imagined.

"I would love to, Clara, but . . . not yet." He added hurriedly, "Right now I'm starving."

She led him around the pianos, picking up Danny's string bass on the way.

Across the dining room table, Marshall pressed the crumbs of pumpkin pie up with the underside of his fork.

Clara had turned on the Shaker hymns her father had been listening to before her family left that morning. The clear voices, singing of gathering and blessings and seasons, drifted in over the speakers that her dad and Danny had wired into the corners of all the rooms.

Besides dessert plates and coffee, all that was left on the table were two long-stemmed wine glasses. Clara had gotten down the good crystal and poured them one-half glass each from the bottle open in the refrigerator. For the last couple of years her parents had served her a glass on big occasions, so she knew they wouldn't mind.

He had helped clear and had loaded the dishwasher, and she had ground fresh beans for coffee. She hadn't asked him about the coffee; it just seemed like the thing to do for a twenty-year-old man. It must have been, because he was on his third cup. She had thought about pretending to be a coffee drinker herself, sneaking half-cups down the sink when he wasn't looking. But she didn't. She poured herself just a little, with an equal part of milk, and barely sipped it.

The dining room was in the middle of the house, separated by archways to the den, the kitchen, and the music room on three sides. There was a fireplace on the fourth side and her dad had built a fire. "To keep you company," he had said. Clara smiled to herself. She didn't think this was the kind of company he'd imagined.

She had lit the candles her mother kept on the table, even though she could hear the Maestra's voice reminding her that it wasn't proper to dine by candlelight during the day. She had felt a little embarrassed to do it, as if she might be making too big a deal of things. But it was Thanksgiving. And the light, reflecting off the cut crystal, was lovely.

The talk had been easy. Laughing, they had rated the worst of the PSOs—piano-shaped objects—in the practice rooms. They told audition stories—performing the Chopin D-flat Prelude on a piano without a D-flat. There were games guessing pieces from the first sung measure, or from hands landing on the tablecloth in the position of the first chord. She had guessed the Liszt that way, and he had gotten the Appassionata from the first single C notes.

There had been other talk, too. Of parents. Tashi. His journal of poetry and houseful of sisters. Danny, and Holly, whom he remembered from McDonald's as the girl with

Band-Aids on her palms and green and white nail polish on her fingers.

But now there was no talk, just the flickering fire and candles, and the Shaker hymns.

Marshall looked her in the eye. "Would you play for me?"

She turned the Thanksgiving music off mid-hymn. Now there was only the pop of the fire and the aroma of the burning piñon.

Clara went to the black Yamaha. She would need its brightness. Marshall stayed in his chair, behind her at an angle.

She hadn't opened the shutters and the music room was shadowy. It felt right, and she left the piano light off. She wouldn't need it because she would play from her repertoire. She didn't want pages getting between her and the notes.

Resting one hand on the black lacquer, she turned to him. "Rachmaninoff, Prelude in G Minor."

He would know she was showing off a little. He nodded his approval.

Clara began softly. It was a lilting march with athletic technical demands. Her hands had to be quick to maintain the strict rhythms of the detached staccato chords, building accents, and alternating majors and minors. By the time she reached the first double forte with its measure of double-octave sixteenth-note chords, her fingers were sweating on the keys.

The accents became dissonant, and the rhythms gave over their place to the relieving interlude. The tension between

Clara's fingers and the notes fell away as the melodic line moved over the rising and falling phrases in the lower ranges. Finally, as if reluctant to leave, the melodies slowed, and the march, not to be denied, reentered.

The theme crept in more quietly this time, but it quickly expanded to fortes and double fortes as it moved toward the inevitable. Clara held back the final crescendo. The temptation was to overdo it, but if she gave too much too soon there would be no place to go and she would kill it. The explosion came one fraction of a moment after the last possible fraction of a moment, resolving itself into massive chords while the theme blasted forth. It sounded like four pianos playing at once. The chords hurt her wrist, but she refused to back off.

There was a diminuendo, a quick leggiero, and then Clara's fingers lifted off the keys. She put her hands in her lap. She knew it was the best she had ever played.

Behind her, he got slowly up.

He placed one candlestick on the ledge of the Yamaha, where its reflection flickered in the underside of the lid, and carried the other around with him to Clara's father's piano. He laid the music rack back, clearing his view, and they faced each other under the lifted backs of the instruments.

The notes were simple. He hadn't announced the piece, but he didn't need to. Every pianist had played Robert Schumann's "Kinderscenen," Scenes from Childhood.

The first was a quiet melody, "About Strange Lands and People," with all four repeats, each of them somehow softer. His body moved with the notes. Since Clara was little,

Tashi had trained her not to move when she played. "Don't let the emotion escape through your body. Squeeze every drop out through only your fingertips." But Marshall moved—not a lot, not a detraction, an addition. Clara wondered whether Tashi let him move because it suited him, which it clearly did, or whether he moved in spite of Tashi's instructions, because he had to.

Next was the fifth from the cycle, "Perfectly Contented." Pieces this well known were risky because artists could be criticized for not meeting expectations, or for exactly and tiredly meeting them. Clearly, Marshall wasn't concerned. Nor did he need to be. The songs sounded brand-new, as if Schumann had just jotted the notes in and handed the pages to him to try.

Clara realized these pieces were the farthest possible thing from what she had chosen, as was his playing. If hers was the precise angle of cut crystal flashing in the light, his was the warm glow of a candle through bone china. If hers was long-stemmed red roses, his was garden roses, on a trellis, still growing. She was searching to find words that would tell it, but she stopped. No words could tell it.

Marshall's playing was not scaled up to show what the piano or the pianist could do. It was to show nothing, to just be. It was fresh and lovely in a way that Clara's was not, and at that moment, she knew it.

"Almost Too Serious," number ten, and he smiled at her through the space. The reprieve of the fast allegro scherzando "Blindman's Buff," then back to the quiet "At the Fireside." He was mixing them up, playing them as they came. Spontaneous. Easy. None of them more than a page. The coloring was all pastels, somewhere between soft and extra-soft. Such little songs, under such big hands.

Finally, the solemn, hymn-like half notes of "The Poet Speaks." It would be the last piece. There was nothing that could follow it.

He spoke to her over the strings. "Schumann wrote to his wife about these pieces."

Clara waited.

"'You will like them,' he told her, 'but you must forget that you are a virtuoso.'"

"Did you know I am named for Clara Schumann?"

"And did you know," he answered, still looking at her, "Clara Schumann was named for light and brilliance and clarity?"

He closed his eyes. He was hearing something, but she wasn't sure what until he began the piano solo. It was the Beethoven concerto, and he had been listening to the orchestra introducing the Allegro con brio.

Clara came in two measures later with the answering phrase, exactly on top of his notes. He kept playing but looked up, surprise on his face, as if he hadn't thought of playing in unison.

"I doubt it's exactly what Tashi had in mind," she said over the music.

He grinned. Tashi would have intended lots of starts and stops and running commentary, nothing played through.

Clara kept going, pushing his tempo up to her own slightly faster and lighter version. Occasionally they made comments to each other, noting dynamics or phrasings. When they got to the first break, where the instruments played and the piano rested, Marshall sang the orchestral melody, then nodded her in on the scale. They landed perfectly together on the quiet dolce.

In spite of the number of hours Clara had lived with the concerto, playing it this way, with four hands moving up and down on exactly the same keys at exactly the same moment, made it new. The sound of the notes going out and coming back created a different dimension for the music. Competition rules specified which of the cadenzas to the first movement was to be performed, and they played the solo as a duet, in unison. The final forte chords fell exactly on top of each other, two sets of strings vibrating as one.

They began the second movement, a serene Largo in A-flat major. This time Clara took Marshall's tempo.

"Have you tried a half-pedal on the long decoration?" she asked as they neared the extended impressionistic phrase. "I like it better than a full." Pressing the footpad only partway down suspended the notes with less muddying of the melody. Marshall tried it and nodded.

Clearly, the Largo was his favorite movement. By the coloring of his phrases and the subtle stretching of his rubatos, he was revealing a more romantic side of the music than Clara's more disciplined, classical interpretation allowed.

Now they hardly had to look at their hands; there were no big skips or chords in this movement. They had stopped talking, and their eyes locked over the strings as their hands moved together in the gray shadows, up and down and over the keys. The last A-flats faded, and they sat still, looking at each other, hearing the woodwinds drift away with the notes.

After a long moment, she sensed him putting his hands back on the keyboard. She put hers there too, getting set for the playful final movement, the Rondo.

He winked at the exact moment he started in on the quick thirds, leaving her completely behind and laughing. "God, Marshall!"

It was marked Allegro scherzando, and different editors marked the quarter note from 132 to 144 on the metronome. Clara played it even faster, but Marshall was taking it at what must have been at least two more notches up from that. It was too fast to make sense, but it sounded like fun and she jumped in with him.

Now she had to keep her eyes on the keys. It was like sledding: cold and fast and almost out of control, up and down the hills of scales and broken chords. At the end of the runs of building C majors a "whoa" escaped from her lips and she knew that Marshall's eyes would be laughing if she could have looked, but she couldn't. It was breakneck speed, and it was over before it should have been.

Marshall stood quickly and Clara did too, smiling and breathless. He was walking toward her, but he wasn't smiling, wasn't breathless. There was a different look on his face, an intent look. They met at the side of the two pianos. His hand reached toward her, and this time he did not stop it. Carefully he tucked her hair back behind her shoulder—once on the left, once on the right.

She knew the two times he had touched her before: the coins in her open palm at McDonald's; today, when he put Tashi's shoebox into her hands. But since that first necessary tap in front of the bulletin board, she had never touched him back.

Now she did. She reached up and put her hands around his neck and looked into the green eyes.

He put his mouth on hers. The stubble on his cheek was rough and gritty, like windblown sand. His lips were soft and gentle. But then he wrapped his arms around her and the feeling changed. She didn't know how something could feel strong and needy at the same time, they seemed like opposites, but that was how he felt. She knew, because it was the same way her own body was feeling.

Marshall left. Said he thought he should. Besides, there really was no choice. Not because of Tashi expecting him back, or Clara's parents. They had to practice. They had to put this relationship off four more days.

Clara couldn't sit still on the piano bench. She went to her room and took her jogging clothes off the bedposts.

The sky was a sharp blue. She pulled a knit cap out of the pocket of her sweats and stretched it over her ears. She tucked her key—cold—between her flattened breasts. Usually she walked the first block. Today she started at a dead run.

Her two-mile route followed the white picket fence down the hill, then looped through the park with the footbridge and bandstand, then returned up the hill with the pickets.

Down the first slope, her legs almost ran away with her. The cushions in her shoes felt springy and new. At the footbridge, she leaped over the missing planks with a yard to spare, circled the bandstand, and leaped over the missing planks again on the return.

Before she could believe it was possible, Clara was back in front of her house, not even breathing hard. Jogging in place, she took her pulse, as always.

She ran to the end of the block, made a U, and headed back over the same route.

By the end of the second two-mile lap, sweat trickled down the backs of her knees. She shed her sweatshirt and tied it around her waist. Perspiration had seeped through her tank top in a patch on her chest. She stuffed her cap into her waistband and let her hair fly. Salty drops fell from her eyebrows into her eyes. She swiped at them and kept going. She didn't take her pulse this time. She didn't think of taking it.

The next time Clara made a U turn at the end of her street, she was barely aware of it. Somewhere along the route she had stopped counting the miles and the laps and the times she had thudded back and forth across the footbridge. Now, alongside her, the landmarks simply came and went.

The bridge, the bandstand, the bridge again . . .

Marshall's playing sounded in her head.

Kinderscenen.

He was going to win.

This is my third try at the Nicklaus.

His last chance.

I wanted to come only if she thought I had a shot at winning.

Kinderscenen. Such little songs, under such big hands.

He was going to win. And it was right for him to.

The pickets running up the hill . . . White stake after white stake after white stake. White key after white key after white key. Scales, running up and down the keyboard.

A little girl is practicing scales. Maybe nine years old. Under her, the bench is cold. The house is dark because it is very early. The little girl keeps looking at the timer.

The timer on the scoreboard says there are only seconds to go. The chocolate is hot, and the band is sweetly out of tune, and she feels good with someone's arm around her—even if it is the wrong someone's. *Was this what ordinary life would be like? If she didn't play?*

The little girl is eleven now. Still practicing those scales. Still casting glances at the red digits.

Did the little girl have doubts? Even then?

Clara's feet were hot and swollen and tight inside her shoes, her socks wet, rubbing blisters. Ahead, the pickets rose up in front of her.

She was okay with Marshall's winning.

And not just because he deserved it. Because she didn't know if she wanted to win anymore.

From here on out, she would only be going through the motions.

But she would go through the motions as diligently as she could. He was entitled to a real win over his closest challenger. And hearing the two of them play, one after the other—and knowing she had prepared to the best of her ability—well, it was the only way her parents and Tashi would see the truth.

Clara's legs pumped under her. Her hair was matted and the tops of her ears were frozen brittle. Her elbows flailed and every breath seared her lungs, but she didn't break stride.

She gritted her teeth and followed the pickets up the final slope. Whatever number of miles she was on, she was going to finish.

At ten o'clock Clara's family returned and found her the way they had left her, bent over the keyboard in her jeans and ballet shoes. They had brought cold turkey, and her dad made her a sandwich.

The only thing out of the ordinary was the melted candles on the dining room table. Her mother would notice, and Clara had thought about replacing them with fresh ones. But she decided not to. Instead, she told her parents about Marshall's coming over.

They looked surprised, and Clara hurried to explain that Tashi had sent him, that they had eaten, and practiced—

Her mother cut her off. "No explanation necessary, sweetheart. We trust you. And you've been working so hard. I'm just glad you had some Thanksgiving."

Friday was her rehearsal with Tashi. After the all-day session, her wrist hurt some. She wrapped it that night, took three aspirin—one more than the bottle said—and forgot about it. Saturday was practice while Marshall had his all-day lesson.

By Sunday, she knew the schedule was right because there was nothing left to do. Clara set the timer for two hours. She worked technique and sight-read some Haydn. She played the concerto once through slowly, concentrating on every note. The only section she worked was the one with the new fingering. She checked the big skips, jumping off one chord and landing on the next. Three minutes to go. She played the Maninov piece, "The Little Daughter of the Snow," and finished with the beeper.

Third Movement

Tucked in a fetal position, Clara listened to the morning sounds passing through the wall: the toaster, rattling newspapers, the *Today* show. They were sounds she usually never heard because she was practicing.

The click of her mother's shoes approached. There was a pause when she picked up the string bass, and then another when she set it down.

"Are you up, sweetheart?" She knocked gently.

"I'm up," Clara called back, not moving.

"Your dress is on the back of the door and we're leaving to take Danny to school. I'm going in to make a few calls, then Dad and I are running errands. We'll be back for you at eleven-thirty."

Clara suspected they were manufacturing the errands to give her time alone.

The clicks receded. "Mom," Clara shouted after her, sitting up. The clicks returned. "I'd like to wear your ruby earrings."

"Of course, sweetheart. They'll be good with the dress."

By the time Clara got back from her two miles, she had the house to herself. She shed a trail of clothes to the bathroom and turned the shower on hot.

Steam piled up behind the plastic curtain. She did the repeat shampoo, which she usually never did, then massaged in conditioner. Maybe she should do a second condition, too—it might add some shine. She worked some more into her hair, then shaved her legs with a brand-new blade. Finally she stepped out, wrapped a towel around her chest, and wiped a hand across the mirror.

She scrubbed her teeth, spit, scrubbed again. She checked her smile. Odd—the gap didn't bother her so much anymore. She wouldn't say that it was her hold on one-of-a-kind beauty, but she didn't think it totally sabotaged her, either. Arranging the white plastic end of the toothbrush behind it, the way she always did—or used to—she envisioned the gap not there. There was something not right about that. Still, she'd have it fixed. Probably.

She blew her hair dry to a satiny sheen, then brushed it away from her face. A French braid would be less adolescent than wearing it loose. She separated the strands, wound them over and under, and clipped a small black velvet bow to the end.

She swabbed her face with astringent, then rubbed in untinted Clearasil. Listening in her head as Tashi played the orchestral introduction, she came in with the piano solo. C chord, root position in the bass, first inversion in the treble, the little decoration, landing on the G7, the answering phrase decorating the D, back to the C.

She brushed her eyebrows up. She did have good eyebrows. Full and dark and she never had to pluck them.

Climbing C major to the D, G7, C . . . She stroked on a wispy line of eyeliner—which still wasn't very much makeup, considering that she would be onstage—and brushed her lashes with two coats of clear-shine mascara. Wow. The mascara changed her. Those big, serious eyes.

Quick triplets, top notes building a C chord . . . She dabbed powder on her face, then sifted it away with the brush. Her skin was extra-clear today. Her period was last week, so that was good—good for her skin, her weight, her mood, everything.

No lipstick. There was lots of color without it and she just slicked on moisturizer. C, D, G7, C, the double forte broken C major chord rolling down the keyboard.

Already nine forty-five. Still singing the notes in her head, she went to the kitchen and got out cereal and milk. Her eyes jumped from headline to headline. She folded the newspaper and put it away.

On her way to her bedroom she picked up her jogging clothes. She hooked them over the bedposts, smoothed her quilt, then stretched flat on her back and gazed up at the ballet posters tacked to the ceiling. It was already five after ten. It took exactly fifty-five minutes to "say" the piece through if she did it on brain-power alone, not allowing her fingers to move. She closed her eyes. She couldn't be looking at ballet posters if she was going to finish.

At eleven she got up. She had done it carefully, exactly, skipping nothing.

She opened a package of pantyhose and took the red dress out of its plastic. Zipped, she stood back from the mirror. Seventeen years' worth of autographed symphony tickets were in the way. She pulled them out of the frame and tossed them on the bed.

It was a tailored, form-fitting wool crepe, sleeveless, with a jacket. She had bought it with her own money so there couldn't be any arguments. Her mother must have been surprised at the color because Clara always wore neutrals. But she had nodded and said, "Wonderful choice, Clara, exactly right. And the jacket will be perfect to slip on for the reporters."

Clara lifted her music satchel off the knob of her bed. She put in a second package of hose. Wallet, keys, money for the Coke machine. Kleenex and Chapstick. White cotton gloves and one of Danny's baby spit-up cloths, folded and pressed like a handkerchief, for her hands. A Bit-O-Honey. Her ballet slippers and ragg socks with the toes and heels cut out so she could take off her shoes in Tashi's office. Aspirin.

She carried the satchel into the music room, flipped through the soft pages of the Beethoven, then dropped it in. Not that she would be needing it. But it was important to have it with her. Technique books. "Little Daughter of the Snow"—it would be a way to take her mind off things if she was nervous. Paper and pencil for notes during the other performances. The little digital timer, set to clock mode, because she wasn't wearing a watch.

She buckled the satchel down tight and laid it out with her jacket and coat and winter gloves. It was eleven-twenty. They would be here in minutes, a planned fraction early.

In the den, she went to her mother's jewelry box. Half good jewelry, half not. Even Clara didn't know which was which. Standing at the bureau, Clara slipped in the delicate ruby earrings, then studied her face in her mother's mirror, looking for any resemblance.

The dark hair and eyes, her father's. Her height, her father's. The sprinkling of freckles she shared with Danny. The gap, only hers. Maybe the shape of her face, the perfect oval, was her mother's. Other than that, there was no sign of her.

Her mother. The Maestra. Today was going to be toughest on her. Tashi must know already. She had taught Marshall and knew what he could do. Clara's father would be disappointed, but he would be okay, quiet as usual, worried about Clara and how she was taking it. But her mother.

Although Clara's mother had judged Nicklaus finals in previous years, Marshall had never been one of the finalists, so she had never heard him play. It would be hard for her to hear him, hard to hear the obvious difference. It would be harder still for her to hear Clara's name announced one name too soon. And the realization that she would not be conducting her daughter at the New Year's concert—that would be almost unbearable.

Clara tightened the backs of the earrings. Well, the Maestra was the one who had pushed Clara the hardest, who kept assuming Clara was going to win. To some extent, she had set up her own heartbreak. Her mother was strong; she'd handle it. Maybe that was what they shared.

Her parents pulled into the driveway and honked. It was eleven twenty-eight.

Computer-generated signs hung on the first five practice rooms. RESERVED MARISA STEPHENS SWINSON. RESERVED MARTIN ROBLES REED. RESERVED

HAROLD WONG. RESERVED MARSHALL HAMMONDS LAWRENCE. Marshall would be in number 12, not here. RESERVED CLARA ALEXANDER LORENZO.

She headed for the stairs. She'd hang out in Tashi's office and practice there. Access to Tashi's comfortable space was one advantage she had.

At two minutes before twelve, according to the clock in the bottom of her satchel, Clara slipped into her aisle seat beside Tashi, who sat beside her parents. They were saving seats for Danny and Holly. The auditorium was already half full with family and friends, university music students, journalists from the music magazines, and someone, somewhere, from the *New York Times.* The five judges—with empty seats separating them—were three rows ahead. She didn't see Marshall.

At twelve noon Marisa Swinson's accompanist began the orchestral introduction. By the first fifty measures Clara could tell that this candidate wasn't a contender. There was something "finger proud," as Tashi would say, about her playing—all machinery, no content. Clara didn't like competitions where they all had to play the same piece, but she had to admit that it was telling.

Clara waited until the movement was over, then slipped out. People would be coming and going all day, and it wasn't necessary to wait until the end of the piece if you moved quietly. She climbed the stairs to Tashi's office and made tea.

At one twenty-five she came down again. Martin Reed was already starting the Rondo. He had been in her program section, so she had already heard him play. He was very good, and except for the gap between their scores at this point, he could have given both Marshall and her a real run. Probably she was listening to third place, Clara thought. But he was good enough that it was giving her butterflies, so she left.

Upstairs she practiced the big skips, the initial tempos. She took her flats off and put the stretched-out ballet shoes on, layering the ragg socks over. She would start her exercises at two, then go down and listen to Marshall at three, and come back up to Tashi's for the short break. She'd collect herself and play over the little section with the new fingering one last time. It would mean going on without having played the concerto today. But playing it through was useless, and the best hope for spontaneity after all the days of practice was to play it for the first time onstage.

Outside Tashi's window, students roamed the quad. Clara assigned them majors. The philosophy students were the ones with the long hair and the pipes. That was so ridiculous, kids with pipes. Even professors with pipes were ridiculous. The accounting and business majors were easy. Knit shirts, tucked in and pressed. Probably there were pre-med and pre-law and all sorts of majors out there milling around, more majors than Clara even knew about. Was that where she belonged? Out there in the quad, instead of up here in Tashi's fourth-floor office like Rapunzel in her tower?

The time had gotten away from her, and she realized she had missed the third finalist, Harold Wong, altogether, which was unfortunate because she had not heard him before. There was just time to complete her warmup before she went down to hear Marshall.

Thinking about Marshall made her jittery. She hadn't seen him, but she knew where he must be, five floors beneath her. Maybe she would feel less restless if she ran down. She would just walk by the door, not interrupt. Make sure some tragedy had not befallen him and that he was at least in the building.

Clara quit the E-flat scale mid-run. Without putting her shoes on—her ballet shoes would be quieter and no one would see her anyway—she walked quickly down the empty hall toward the stairs.

Except for the first five rooms, deserted now because the first and second competitors had played and the third was onstage, the lights were off, even the hall light. But thank God, she could see the rectangle of yellow on the linoleum in front of number 12.

Muffled piano music reached her before she was halfway there. "Rhapsody in Blue." He would like Gershwin, be good at that jazzy stuff. But why would he be playing Gershwin now? And the Rhapsody? It was so overplayed.

She passed quickly by the window, glimpsing the neat ponytail, tied today with a leather string, then stood to the side, her back to the music coming through the soundproofing. He rode out a scale and ended it in a Scott Joplin rag. After a minute the rag slowed, and dissolved into "Maria," a love song from *West Side Story,* which turned into "I'm Dreaming of a White Christmas."

God, Broadway songs and Bing Crosby? Well, he might

be certifiable but at least he was here. She tiptoed back upstairs and started arpeggios.

Ever since she had played the Rachmaninoff for Marshall, her wrist had been hurting more. Today it was much worse than usual. She had already taken two aspirin, but she hopped up and downed a third, then went back to the keyboard.

She had hoped the wrist would have been rested, from just the little bit of practicing yesterday and today, but instead it felt stiff. She favored it on the arpeggios especially, cocking and uncocking her wrist to pass her thumb under. If she supported it, holding her left hand underneath her right, it hurt less, and she practiced that way, one hand at a time.

That was when she realized that Tashi, who had promised to get her when Marshall was up, was standing behind her. Clara's left hand jumped back on the keyboard where it belonged, running along with the right. Keeping the pain out of her face, she completed the exercise.

Clara pulled her cotton gloves on and slipped into the last row. She didn't want to sit with her parents; there was something about Marshall's playing that was just between the two of them. Besides, back here, she could hold her wrist without anyone seeing.

Tashi was already onstage at the second piano. The other accompanists had used music and page-turners, but Tashi thought it was distracting and played from memory.

"Candidate four. Mr. Marshall Hammonds Lawrence."

Clara bolted up straight, looking over the heads of the crowd, wondering where he would come from and what he would be wearing. She hadn't stayed in front of the tiny window long enough to see anything except the back of a white shirt.

The side door opened and Marshall walked in smiling, a black handkerchief in his hand. He was wearing a suit with a small print—probably houndstooth, though she couldn't be sure from where she was—and a banded collarless shirt. He bounded up the stairs to the stage, then stopped to kiss Tashi's hand, a gesture that brought smiles all around.

Clara stretched to see him full length. Black shoes, maybe wingtips, new; he hadn't had any dress shoes lined up on his sleeping bag. The clothes must have taken a month's pay, but she had to admit they were worth it.

After what seemed like an eternity, Tashi began.

The first movement went beautifully—though Clara was so scared she could barely listen. She could see her mother and father whispering, heads together.

There was a pause and he began the second movement—the Largo, his favorite.

This one's all yours, Marshall, she thought, barely breathing. Only four measures in and her palms were wet under the cotton gloves.

The notes were round and mellow, the interior voices singing—

Then *bang!* Like a faraway gunshot. Even Tashi looked up, surprise on her face.

Clara knew the sound. His foot had slipped off the pedal,

and the brass had popped up against the wood frame. He went on, but without the pedal, the glassy, varnished quality of the tones was shattered, and the gliding decoration that was supposed to last the long measure was gone.

The audience stirred. The judges marked their papers. Marshall's face turned ashen.

Clara put her head in her gloves.

He had been trying the half-pedal, the way she had told him when they played the Largo together. Why had she ever shown it to him? Days before was too late to be experimenting—Tashi had said so, and Clara knew it too. Or maybe he had been thinking of her, the way they had played the slow movement together. She hoped not. He would hate her forever if it had been that. Maybe it was just the new shoes. Maybe he had forgotten to put masking tape on the soles so they wouldn't slip.

It was the kind of thing that could happen; the judges would understand that. A popped-up pedal didn't necessarily mean he wouldn't win, he just had to immediately recover, show them what he could do. Head still in her hands, Clara tried to listen. But the playing sounded muffled and far away . . .

She stayed through the third movement. It was hard, but she owed him that.

He looked fine through her watery eyes. Handsome and composed, smiling even, when he took his bow.

She couldn't say how long it had taken him to recover, or if he ever had, or how the Rondo had gone. She didn't know. She had barely heard at all. She had been thinking of her own choices.

Turn. Five steps to Tashi's shelves, stuffed with albums and tapes and CDs. Turn. Five steps to the window and the quad through the wavy glass. Turn . . .

There were three possibilities.

One. Drop out. Just never show up down there, on the stage. Or go to the judges, tell them she needed to withdraw. Unthinkable. Not a real choice.

Two. Throw the competition. Purposely goof, or fake a blank-out—something the judges could not overlook. Make sure Marshall won. But it would be a lie.

Three. Play and win and go to Juilliard. Practice all day and perform all night for the rest of her life.

Nineteen minutes to decide.

Tashi appeared in the doorway. "So." She looked over the tops of her glasses. "Clara, my darling, there is something I wish to tell you."

Clara continued to pace, hands on hips.

"It is important that you hear. Before you play." Tashi disappeared into the piano room.

Whatever it is, Tashi, not now.

"Remember?" Tashi reappeared, her glasses swinging. "'I will tell you,' I said, the night you hurt your arm." She held the crystal snow-globe.

God, Tashi.

"I know, you are thinking it isn't the time." She settled herself on the couch.

"Tashi," Clara said sharply, "you could have told me the story of that snow-globe any day for the last fourteen years. I don't think today is the day."

"But it is."

Tashi tipped the snow-globe over and up, then settled it in her lap. "Shostakovitch . . . Prokofiev . . . Khachaturian . . . others you would not know. They were Soviets, Clara, and they were the greats, but as a young girl I was not always allowed to play them.

"People said it would be better after Stalin died. And it was. Still, every program, every selection, had to be approved . . . "

Clara was hardly listening.

"We bought music on the black market. We practiced quietly, so the wrong person, walking by, under a window, would not hear. Clara, can you even imagine—being afraid to do what you were born to do?

"Khrushchev came along, and suddenly the Party wanted tours to the West. And so we began to travel.

"There was a man—a friend—at the Moscow Conservatory."

Clara still paced, but she was suddenly alert. It was the first time Tashi had ever mentioned a man in her life.

"This man, he understood how I suffered. The day I left for the Paris tour, he went with me in the limousine. You see, I could tell no one what I was about to do, not even my parents or my brothers and sisters. They could be sent to the Gulag—the work camps, in Siberia—if they knew. I could not even tell . . . my friend. He had to be able to answer truthfully. But he knew. I was not coming back."

Tashi's voice dropped. Clara's walking slowed.

"On the way to the airport, in the back of the limousine, my friend slipped this globe from under his overcoat. As long as I had known him, it had decorated the ledge of his piano at the conservatory. It had been saved, somehow, by his mother—from before the Revolution, when people still had such things."

Clara watched her.

"'To remember,' Mikhail said. 'May it bring you courage.'" Tashi's bosom heaved a shuddery sigh.

"So." Her voice returned to level and she looked up at Clara. "At the airport they checked everything. No pictures. No extra suitcases. It would have been suspicious. 'The globe,' I said, 'it is just a gift,' and I kept my hands around it, inside my muff, all the way to Paris."

Arms at her sides, Clara stood listening.

"The next morning, hours before dawn, I slipped out of my Paris hotel and away on the cobblestones. It was still dark—I was drinking coffee at the American Embassy—when the cable came from Washington. 'Bring her in quickly,' the telegram said. 'Asylum will be granted.'"

Clara sat down on the couch beside Tashi. "Why didn't you ever go back?" she asked gently. "You could, couldn't you, now? I mean, there isn't even a Soviet Union anymore."

Tashi looked down at the snow-globe.

"I don't mean go back for good," Clara added hastily. "I mean just to visit, to find your parents, your brothers and sisters. Maybe your—friend."

"How little you understand, Clara. It was 1962, the middle of the Cold War. Letters and calls to or from the West were evidence of spying. No, I have heard nothing in thirty-six years. I am quite sure my parents are dead, my brothers and sisters lost to me."

"But you don't know. You could trace them." Clara was talking faster. "The State Department would help you, I bet. And your friend. You could find out about him from the conservatory—"

"I'm sure he has forgotten all about the young pianist in the back of the limousine."

"He hasn't forgotten Natalia Petrovna Volkonskaya," Clara said firmly. "The whole world knows Natalia Petrovna Volkonskaya."

"Enough, Clara. Put out your hands."

She had told the story, though Clara still had no idea why she had chosen this incredible moment, and now they were getting back to business. Probably Tashi was going to check the temperature of her fingers. But instead, Tashi put the crystal snow-globe into them. She wrapped her spotted hands around Clara's smooth ones, weaving a nest. "I wish you to have it."

"Tashi, I couldn't."

"Clara, this is one thing about which you do not have a choice." She looked straight into Clara's eyes. "May it bring you courage."

Tashi was already at the second piano when Clara peeked from the wings.

She scanned the crowd for Marshall's broad shoulders but didn't find them. The faces of the judges, sitting in the roped-off row, gave away nothing. Four had flown in from Juilliard and one was the concertmaster of the Philharmonic, substituting on the panel for Clara's mother, who was disqualified this year.

Clara found her parents, fidgeting. Next to them, taking off their coats, sat Danny and Holly.

Danny and Holly. The oddest memory came to her, of the three of them. Clara and Holly were sitting on the park footbridge dangling their legs over the side when Danny, not more than eight, ran up shouting. There was a rusted coffee can in his hands and in the bottom was a little water turtle.

The three of them talked about Danny's terrarium, and about how the turtle would never go hungry and always be safe. They talked about wildlife and habitats and freedom. They talked until it got dark.

Finally, it was Clara's idea: they fixed the can, half in and half out of the creek, weighting it with stones in the cold water. The angle was exactly halfway—maybe the turtle would swim out during the night, maybe he wouldn't. They would come back in the morning and see what God had decided . . .

Let God decide. It was the answer. Clara had been suffering over a choice she didn't even have to make.

If she refused to play, or messed up on purpose, that would be making it her decision. But if she just went out there and played normally, that would be leaving it to fate—

to what was supposed to happen, ordained to happen.

Tashi's voice: *Be glad your nap came early, and not at a time when it really mattered.* Maybe today was the time that really mattered. Maybe a memory lapse had been foreshadowed way back then . . .

Or the new fingering might throw her. Jesus, the new fingering. Tashi's story had distracted her and Clara had forgotten to go over the new fingering. Maybe that was fate, too.

Or maybe her sore wrist would interfere. Of course—the wrist was a sign she was on the right track. There had been no loose board in the dance floor, no stray bobby pin. Fate had tripped her, that night at rehearsal. It was fate's way of keeping her a hair under top condition, of making sure there wasn't a mistake in the big overall plan and that she didn't accidentally win.

There were thousands of fateful things that could intervene—if they were supposed to. Thousands . . .

Clara pulled off her gloves and folded them over the curtain pulley. "Please hold the wing curtain back for me," she whispered to the music student who had crept backstage for a better view. "I am going to start from the wall. Back there." She pointed. "So when the audience sees me come from behind the curtains, I will already be in full stride."

"Candidate five. Miss Clara Alexander Lorenzo."

Clara strode past the music student and onto the stage. Applause broke out at her appearance.

The crystal snow-globe was in her upstage hand. Quickly,

she placed it to the right of the high keys, where it would be hidden from the audience. Laying her hand lightly on the piano, she acknowledged the crowd with a dip of her head. She put the cloth inside the lip of the piano just forward of the strings, and set the bench. She turned the knob to adjust the seat from Marshall's height and without pausing gave Tashi the nod.

The second piano began the introduction to the first movement.

God, her wrist was suddenly killing her, and she wasn't even playing yet. Sweat popped out on her forehead.

Clara reached for her cloth, dabbed her fingers and face, folded it, and put it back.

Page three, the piano solo entered.

Her fingers were moving, but her brain didn't click in the way it should have. The pain was stealing her focus. She tried to think about the notes, but that made her think about playing them, which made her think about the pain. She was drifting.

Sometimes it happened during practice or at a lesson, and Clara would be surprised to find herself at the end of a piece. It was like reading a book to the bottom of the page and having no idea what the words had said. But she had never drifted during a performance. It was dangerous. More than dangerous. Tashi said unfocused playing was like flying an airplane without checking the fuel: you could fall from the sky at any moment.

Clara tried to listen, to hear whether a memory lapse was coming. Sometimes she could hear them coming when other people played. She heard nothing. No lapse. No absence of a lapse.

Help me, Tashi, she thought over the keys, and Tashi's gentle voice answered. *In practice, question every note. In performance, never question even one.*

She forced herself to say the names of the notes in her head—this was the very thing it was for, to protect her. She might even be whispering, she wasn't sure, but she thought her lips were moving.

Lord, it hurt! Think of Marshall. Then maybe it wouldn't hurt. Suddenly she wished she knew where he was.

They were talking, her brain was playing tricks on her. *God, Marshall, playing Gershwin and Joplin and show songs before the biggest competition of your life?* He shrugged. *Why not? They're wonderful songs.*

She knew what he meant. It was the same feeling she'd had when she danced, improvising in the spotlight to the saxophone music. Pure movement, pure joy, not caring what anyone thought.

The same way he didn't care that his songs were clichés. Clichés became clichés because they were good, right? So good that people fell in love with them and played them or danced them to death.

The Nutcracker . . . This time it was Clara's mother's voice that came to her. *It's . . . well, a Christmas show. A cliché.* Clara's answer. *And so what if it is.*

She had been so right, and she hadn't even known it. So what if it is, if you have a passion for it.

Passion. Had she ever truly had a passion for piano? Tashi

had said, "You seemed to be having a very good time." But a very good time for a three-year-old was fun, not passion.

Jesus, my hand hurts. Please, God, don't let me think about my hand anymore.

She'd played passionately the afternoon she and Marshall were together. Today, in the practice room, his playing had sounded the same way it had that day. Probably his playing sounded like that every day. It did, she suddenly knew, because that was the way you were supposed to feel every time. My God, that was the way you were supposed to feel every time! And she had felt that way only once, in her whole life. And then it had been because of Marshall, not the piano.

Clara felt a cold chill. Tashi whispered in her ear. *Perhaps it will add that certain something*. Now she knew what.

Page 29, the second movement.

She had no business being here, doing this. Because if you didn't love, really love, the piano, no amount of fame or money or even romance would make the days and days of practice endurable. They would be eternity. Eternity in hell—no, that was wrong, piano had never made her miserable. The eternal days of practice would be neither joyful nor hellish. They would be long.

Clara watched her hands moving over the keyboard. Her wrist didn't hurt anymore, or maybe it did and she just didn't feel it. She no longer tried to name the notes in her head. She was detached, watching from above.

Then she noticed the oddest thing. Maybe it was the pain or the extra aspirin because she must be hallucinating. Otherwise, why hadn't she seen when she first sat down?

The keys. Keys just like the keys she had stared at three hours a day for the past fourteen years. Eighty-eight keys that she had always thought were black and white. They were, weren't they?

Suddenly she wasn't sure. Because the keys that the girl in the red dress were playing were not black and white. They were gray.

Not light gray, not dark gray. They were exactly halfway between black and white. They weren't gray the way they were in the music room at five-thirty in the morning when she practiced in the dark because the piano light hurt her eyes. They weren't gray the way they were when she and Marshall were alone in the house and she played while he watched from the shadows. No, these keys were truly gray. Someone had come in when she wasn't looking and painted them a flat, even, prison gray. And with no visual cues, the girl in the red dress was groping her way blindly over them.

Funny, she had been proud of herself for being more truthful lately. But what she saw now was that she was still lying.

Yes, the keys were black and white for Marshall. "When I went upstairs the sun was up," he had said. For Marshall everything was black and white.

But for her, for the girl in the red dress, black and white keys were a lie. And she was living the lie, at this very moment, by being up here pretending she could do this for the rest of her life.

Clara placed her hands for the third movement and looked over at Tashi.

There was the slightest dip in one eyebrow. What did Tashi see? Clara nodded her in.

Tashi. Dear, dear Tashi. But she shouldn't have given Clara the snow-globe. Clara stole a sideways look at it, her charm, at the top of the keys.

And why had it been so important for Tashi to tell her the story today, just before she played? There had to be a clue there somewhere.

She had thought about it on the elevator, Tashi holding her gloves and the globe while Clara dabbed at her fingers. May it bring you courage. It had done that for Tashi. Courage to leave her family, her home, her friend, courage to follow her music. So now Tashi was giving it to Clara to bring courage. The courage to play her best. The courage to get through it. It had seemed right in the elevator, but it didn't seem right now.

So, Tashi. Clara's visions were talking again. *What's the courage for?* She stole a glance at the wavy white hair, but Tashi was playing, her eyes on the keyboard, and there was no answer.

What would be the hardest thing for me? The thing for which I would most need courage?

To not play.

Suddenly, she was sure.

Tashi had seen it all along, that something was missing.

She remembered Tashi's description of their first meeting. "Those old halls never heard music as lovely as your laughter." Was she saying that laughter was better even than music? Clara remembered the afternoon in Tashi's office after the splint came off. "Just because the doctor says you can play, it doesn't mean you should . . . Clara, look me in the eyes and tell me . . . Do you yearn to play it?" *Yes.* It was a lie.

She hadn't realized how much of a lie when she had said it. She had wanted to play the concerto. For her parents, for Tashi, for Marshall. Maybe even for the black and white dress that her mother hadn't found yet in the store window. But she had never yearned to play it. What she yearned to do, now, she knew, was quit.

It was almost over. Every note sent knifing pain through Clara's wrist. She tried to keep her face under control, but the pain was making her nauseated. Just two more measures. The final piano notes were quiet and fading, but Clara's hands jumped off the formata at the first possible moment.

Through the entire concerto she hadn't named a single note, but it hadn't mattered because she had not blanked out. As for the new fingering, she had completely forgotten to notice when the section went by. She didn't know if she had used the new or the old, but there had been no trip-up.

She had played in some kind of altered state, not with emotion, surely nowhere close to her best. The judges would hear this, and the competition would go to Marshall in spite of his slip. Which was what Clara knew now, with certainty, was supposed to happen.

She stood up, took a poised step forward, and bent from the waist, arms at her side.

The crowd was on its feet, a few voices shouting "Brava!" and then others joining in.

Keeping the smile on her face that she had carefully arranged there to hide the pain, Clara looked at Tashi. She was smiling broadly, also standing now, back and to the side, motioning Clara to take another bow.

In the middle row, even the judges' heads were appearing, joining the ovation.

Clara turned the sound off. But the house lights were up full and she couldn't not see. The film ran in front of her, row after row of clapping hands.

Her mother and father stepped into the aisle, blowing kisses. Holly had two fingers in her mouth. Danny's fist pumped over his head.

Marshall. She had to find Marshall. There, far to the side in the front row, taller than anyone. He was standing, clapping, slower than the others, looking her in the eye. There was a wistful smile, a resigned look.

Suddenly Clara remembered the end of the story about the little water turtle. The next day, excited to find the turtle still in the can, Clara and Holly and Danny had taken him home to the terrarium. He had lived two days.

She had been wrong to leave it to God.

The judges called a thirty-minute break. People milled in the foyer while the news crews snaked electrical cords between their feet.

Clara stood with her family, her satchel over her shoulder. Using it as a sling, she rested her right arm on top and hoped no one would notice. The snow-globe was deep inside, her ballet shoes and ragg socks tucked around it.

Handshakes were painful, so she substituted hugs. Holly had brought a cooler and popped Cherry Cokes for everyone. Floating through the crowd, Tashi greeted people and occasionally moved back and forth between Clara's group and Marshall, who leaned, alone, against the wall.

"Sweetheart, I'm so proud." Clara's mother gripped her shoulders. "You were everything I knew you would be."

Her dad put his arm around her. "You looked a little pale, I thought, taking your bows."

"The excitement, I guess."

"So what's going on with the wrist?" he asked under the noise, just to her.

She gave a tiny shrug.

Danny grinned at her and she tried to grin back. "I guess you were pretty good. For a meathead."

"Jeez, Clara, I knew you could play"—Holly stopped to switch her wad of gum to her other cheek— "but I didn't know you could play like that." She offered a stick but Clara turned it down; she couldn't be chewing gum in front of the cameras. "Now I get why you were obsessing. I mean, this really is a big deal."

Holly turned her back to Clara's parents. "Now I get Ronald McDonald, too. In those clothes, man"—she fanned her face—"a definite ten. Definitely."

Others came over, including the finalists with their parents and teachers. Everyone was extremely polite, congratulating her on how well she had played. Clara smiled and said thank you and kept her arm on her satchel.

Finally, she sensed Marshall behind her. He put a hand on her waist, tucked her hair back, kissed her on the ear and whispered into it, "It's why I love you."

She took a quick breath. She was watching her parents when he did it. They couldn't have heard, but they could see. They did a good job of keeping the shock out of their faces, but there was that traded look, much longer than usual.

Clara introduced him, and they told him how well he had played. He thanked them, then excused himself. "Very talented young man," her mother offered.

Tashi, unable to break away from the congratulations of her colleagues, hadn't said much to Clara. At last she walked over, took her glasses off, and put her hands on either side of Clara's face. "Excuse us a moment, please," she said, looking into Clara's eyes, "we need to fly away."

Tashi closed the basement door with RESERVED CLARA ALEXANDER LORENZO posted on it, and sat down, her back to the piano.

"So. Come sit." She patted the piano bench, as if she were calling Johann or Sebastian to hop up beside her.

There wasn't room for the satchel between them, so Clara laid it on the floor, being careful of the globe inside. The straps weren't buckled now and her music slid out, but she made no move to collect it.

"What's wrong?" Tashi asked, crossing her arms on her chest.

"You know," Clara said, almost too softly to be heard.

"I don't."

"You have always known."

"Tell me what I have always known."

They sat side by side, staring at the door.

Clara took a big breath. "You have always known I would never be happy as a concert pianist. You have always known I didn't have the passion."

Beside her, there was an intake of air.

"And you should have told me before now, because you have always known, and you really should have told me." The words were coming faster. "And I shouldn't have competed at all and I shouldn't have played today and you should have told me but instead, at the very last minute, you told me that story and gave me the snow-globe to shake me all up inside because you wanted me to realize and quit." The tears were hot on her face.

"No. Absolutely wrong." Without looking at her, Tashi passed a Kleenex, wadded and warm, from her palm.

"But the snow-globe."

"But the snow-globe what?" She sounded annoyed, and for the first time Clara looked at her.

Tashi appeared wavy, as if she were standing behind the old glass in her office window. She didn't look back, she just stared at the door.

"The snow-globe was to bring me courage," Clara said between wipes at her eyes. "Courage to quit."

"No." Now it was much more than annoyance, it was anger in Tahsi's voice. "The snow-globe gives you courage to do whatever it is you need to do. For today, for tomorrow, for the rest of your life. Who am I to say what that would be?"

With her foot Tashi pulled the "Little Daughter of the Snow" music all the way out of the satchel, stamping the blue cover with a print of her pump. Then she stood, sidestepped the music, walked out, and shut the door.

Clara struggled to get control.

She eyed the footprinted blue cover with the snowflakes. She had never seen Tashi treat music that way.

"The Little Daughter of the Snow," by Mikhail Maninov.

Mikhail.

Clara picked up the sheet music, looking for what, she didn't know. Printed on the back page was the children's story by the same title. She thought she had read it early on, but she wasn't sure.

She scanned quickly. She remembered—something about an old couple who wanted a child but couldn't have one. She skipped to the end. There was a signature—presumably Maninov's, though it was in Russian and the letters made no sense to her—and then one sentence in English. "For the one who had to go." Clara turned to the front and checked the copyright. 1962.

The digits blinking up from the bottom of her satchel said there were seven minutes before the announcements. Clara turned back to the story.

Her parents looked relieved when Clara finally slipped into the seat. Her mother passed her the jacket. Tashi, next to her, barely acknowledged her.

The news stations had set up lights in the front of the auditorium, and the chairman of the Nicklaus Committee was on stage with a microphone. "The candidates' scores have been averaged and calculated." There was a complicated system whereby the scores of the First Cut, Second Cut, and final were each given a certain weight. "Names will be called in reverse order," he announced, "the candidate with the highest total score being called last."

One of the judges handed him an envelope. He slipped the card out and read it to himself. "Congratulations to all of them" was all he said.

"Fifth place, with two hundred fifty points, Miss Marisa Stephens Swinson." Marisa Swinson stood up, walked onto the stage, and accepted a certificate. A genuine smile was on her face.

"Fourth place, with two hundred seventy-five points—"

This was a lot of points. It meant things were close at the top.

"—Mr. Martin Robles Reed." A surprise. He was excellent, and Clara had thought he would be third. It meant that Harold Wong, whom Clara had never heard play, was still in the running.

Clara's chest was tightened. She breathed from the top of her lungs.

"Third place, with two hundred ninety points—"

God, *very* close at the top.

"—Mr. Harold Wong."

Looking disappointed, Harold Wong accepted his certificate and a handshake. Clara was gulping air.

"Second place, with two hundred ninety-one points—"

There was only one point's difference between second and third. Please, God, fix this . . .

"—Mr. Marshall Hammonds Lawrence."

Clara sat erect and still. Her mother leaned out over Tashi, her hands gripped together in a prizefighter's cheer. Her dad peeked at her, a huge smile under his salt-and-pepper beard. Danny and Holly bounced in their seats and pretended to stomp their feet on the floor. Only Tashi didn't react.

Onstage, Marshall shook the chairman's hand, took the card, and sat down quickly.

So there hadn't even been a change in order. They were coming out in the same order they had gone in.

"And it is my great pleasure—"

At the skirts of the stage, the news lights came on. The chairman squinted and stopped, then repeated himself for the cameras. "And it is my great pleasure to announce the winner, daughter of our own Ellen Alexander, student of the great Dr. Natalia Petrovna Volkonskaya from our own university—"

Clara didn't like the introduction. And if they were going to do it, they should have announced her father, too.

"—with two hundred ninety-five points—"

It meant she had a perfect score today. The only subtractions had been the reading score at the Second Cut. She didn't know of its having been done before.

"—Miss Clara Alexander Lorenzo."

Clara arranged a smile and stood up. Using her best ballet posture, she walked down the center aisle and up the stairs to the stage. The chairman beamed at her and pumped her hand, sending waves of pain up her arm. He held her lightly at the small of her back and handed her a certificate, which she did not look at. Cameras clicked.

Clara's father followed her path down the aisle. He carried a spray of long-stemmed red roses and lifted it up to her. She took the flowers in her arms and forced a bigger smile. The people were still on their feet.

"Encore! Encore!"

She had never heard of playing an encore at a competition. She looked at the chairman. Surely he would decline for her, explain that it wasn't done, something. But he was standing back, smiling, and motioned toward the piano with his eyes. She searched her father's face. It was expectant.

Clara spread the roses on the floor in front of the piano and the audience sat down. She took her seat—there was no need to adjust it—and waited for a very long time. The crowd cleared their throats and shuffled their feet. She waited for absolute quiet.

She put her fingers on the keys, and a little A-minor melody drifted out from the strings. It was good that there weren't many notes; she didn't think her wrist could have borne many notes.

The audience was stunned; she could hear it. It had been perfectly quiet before she started, but it was more quiet now. They had been expecting something flashy, something like the Rachmaninoff, the stuff of encores.

Clara worked her way through the lighter, brighter middle section, then back to the minor key. She repeated the last section with the soft pedal down, moving the felt hammers so they hit only two of the three strings for each note. If there had been a pedal to shift the hammers another fraction, to hit only one string, she would have used it, but she managed to achieve the sound without it: mournful, the sound of an animal trapped and crying.

They were back on their feet.

She didn't have the energy, but she stood, smiled, and bowed.

Pick up the flowers fast, show them there's no chance of a second encore. Shake the chairman's hand and get off.

They were still clapping. God, weren't they tired of it?

Clara didn't know how she got through the news interviews, with the microphones and video cameras aimed at her. But with her mother and father at her side, she did, and she supposed she said something passable.

The reporter from the *New York Times* was the only one to ask about her choice of an encore. "It means a lot to me" was all Clara said.

They went to dinner at a restaurant that turned at the top of a tower, with a band and a dance floor. Tashi didn't come, and Clara wished the waiter would remove the extra setting. No one argued when Clara said she needed to go home and sleep. She didn't stay up to see herself on the ten o'clock news, but her mom promised to tape it.

The autographed symphony tickets were still piled in the center of her bed. Clara tossed them in the trash and lay down on top of the covers.

The pain was bad and she couldn't sleep. She stared at the dancers on the ceiling and thought about the folktale. All along, the little snow girl had been singing to her, but like the old man and old woman, she had not been able to hear. *Old ones, old ones, I had to go.* If Clara let them keep her wrapped up and close to the fire, she would melt. It was the truth. She was melting already.

Three glasses and an empty champagne bottle were strewn on the dining room table. The front page of the newspaper was conspicuously displayed. There was a picture of Clara at the piano—a professional shot she had submitted with her entrance tape—and an article, which she didn't read.

A scribbled note on a yellow square from her mother's day-planner was gummed to the story. "We love you!" it said. "We left you the Triumph, but don't go to school until you're rested. Mom. P.S. Dad's going to announce it on the PA."

Clara took two aspirin, went into Danny's room, and turned on the computer.

Tashi stood at her door in the iridescent silk robe, Johann and Sebastian panting at her feet. There were purple circles under her eyes, too.

Clara brought the envelope out of her satchel and handed it to her. "I'm sorry, Tashi."

The envelope was addressed to the chairman of the Nicklaus Committee. Tashi kept her eyes on the address and ushered Clara to the dining table. She moved the tea service out of the way and put the envelope in front of her.

Clara gave a little nod, as if she were nodding in the second piano, and Tashi took the letter out. Clara knew the words by heart, and as Tashi read silently, she heard them.

To the Committee:

Please accept my apology for what I am about to write.

I regret to tell you that I must decline the first-place award in this year's Nicklaus Piano Competition. Yesterday, while I played, I realized for the first time that a piano performance career is not right for me. But I felt confused and trapped and didn't know what to do. I have been trying to think about things since then, to clear them up in my head, and now I see that the only thing which makes any sense—for me, and maybe for the committee and Juilliard in the long run—is to decline the award.

I deeply regret the trouble I know this will cause, and I wish it could have happened another way, but I don't think it could have.

Sincerely,

Clara Lorenzo

Clara broke the silence. "I've made an appointment to see the chairman of the committee tomorrow morning."

"Have you told your parents?" Tashi sounded tired.

"No. That's why the letter has to wait until tomorrow. I'm going to tell them tonight."

"Do you want me to be there?"

Tashi's presence would ensure that her parents, her

mother especially, wouldn't go completely berserk. "Thank you, but I don't think so."

Tashi went to the china cabinet for a second cup and saucer, then poured. "Nothing is as bad when you have it with tea."

So it was bad for her, too, even if she thought it was for the best.

Clara sipped while Tashi reread the letter. When she finished she folded it back into the envelope and slid it across the waxed wood.

"So. You are sure."

Clara wished she'd say "my darling."

"I'm sure."

Tashi nodded.

There were things Clara wanted to know, and she tried to begin. "Tashi, why did you come to the Nutcracker rehearsal?"

She sipped her tea. "To see if there was a difference."

"A difference between the way I dance and the way I play. To see if I'm capable of having a passion for anything."

Tashi didn't confirm and she didn't deny, but Clara didn't need her to.

"Tashi, I really am sorry. Sorrier than you know."

"Tell me exactly, Clara"—the gray eyes studied her—"what is it you are sorry for?"

Clara picked up a silver teaspoon and stirred, though she had added nothing to her tea. She stirred for a long time. She wanted to make sure what she said was exactly true.

She wasn't sorry for the years with Tashi. She was happy for that, even if she had missed a lot of other things.

Maybe she shouldn't have played in the competition, but

she didn't regret that she had. It was important to know she had won. That way she knew what she was giving up. And the hurt wrist, the two weeks and two days of nonstop practice, the performance—they were the only way she could have come to see what she had come to see.

She was sorry Marshall would win by her default. It wasn't the way he would want to win, and it would put him off, her handing him the competition that way. And she was sorry for her parents. But those things didn't have anything to do with Tashi.

"I'm sorry," she said finally, "for the things I said to you yesterday in the practice room."

Tashi nodded.

"Thank you," Clara pushed on, "for 'The Little Daughter of the Snow.' I don't know if you gave it to me to help me, or what . . ."

She waited for Tashi to explain, but she didn't.

"But it did. It made me see."

"And what did it make you see?"

Clara thought about all the things she had rolled around in her head during the night. How the piece was Maninov's way of telling Tashi, from behind the Iron Curtain, that he understood that she had to go to her music. How for Clara it meant the opposite, that she had to leave it. But how that was just the beginning, really, of what the piece said. How it spoke to her of parents and children and the assumptions they made about each other, about good intentions and blinding love . . .

But Clara couldn't say all that; it would never come out

right. And she wouldn't presume to interpret the piece for Tashi, the very woman for whom the music had been composed. Besides, Tashi might have her own, different meanings, and they would be just as right. So all she said was, "It made me see what would happen if I didn't stop."

They sipped their tea. Finally, Clara began again. It was the last thing. "Tashi, may I ask you something?"

Tashi raised her eyes, waiting.

"Why, really why, haven't you ever gone back to Russia?"

Now it was Tashi's turn to carefully stir. She added sugar, cream, more sugar, more cream, stirred again. "I am afraid."

"Of the government?"

She humphed. "Of course not of the government. Nothing as small as that." She tinked her teaspoon on the cup. "Afraid to see. Afraid to see my own lovely Russia, afraid to see my brothers and sisters, nieces and nephews, if I have any—"

"Afraid to see Mikhail Maninov?"

Tashi kept her eyes down. "Afraid to see, now, from a distance, whether I made the right choice." Tashi's eyes left the teacup to search for Johann and Sebastian. She found them, curled on the ottoman in the living room. "Because sometimes it is lonely. Because sometimes, my darling, I am not sure."

This brave woman, this artist of artists, wasn't sure?

Clara took the snow-globe out of her music satchel and unwrapped the ragg socks and worn-out ballet shoes. She turned it in her hands, looking for the hairline crack. There. Proof that the globe was real crystal, that it would break. But also proof of its endurance.

"Put out your hands," Clara said.

Tashi set the spoon in the saucer and stretched her hands, spotted and shaky, across the table. How could hands that still played like these shake when she tried to hold them still?

Clara put the snow-globe into them and wrapped her own hands around her teacher's. Tashi's fingers were cold and Clara pressed her flesh against them, wishing she could pass some of her warmth, some of her youth.

"I wish you to have it." As she said it, Clara bent down, trying to see into the gray eyes, hoping Tashi would recognize her own formal syntax and would smile.

But Tashi's eyes were on the hands. "No, Clara, I gave it to you."

"Tashi, this is one thing about which you do not have a choice."

At last Tashi's eyes dared to find her, and Clara saw that they were wet and full.

Clara squeezed tighter. "May it bring you courage."

She checked in at the school office. It seemed like the thing to do; she had a lot of work to make up. One of the secretaries congratulated her, so her dad must have announced it. She just said thank you.

"Welcome back to the dull, everyday world." Holly spritzed cologne behind each ear, then pulled out the front of her sweater and spritzed once where there would have been cleavage if she'd had any. "Hey, did you know I got on the news last night, standing behind you?"

"Great. That's great."

She pointed the bottle toward Clara. "Wanna spray? To celebrate?"

"I'm not celebrating," Clara said, already writing in her spiral ring. "I'm working on my Lit paper and I'm turning down the Nicklaus."

"Clara, I don't know why I even hang with you, you never party and you never get loose and you're what?"

"I'm turning down the Nicklaus."

The bottle slipped through Holly's fingers and splintered. Raspberry fumes wafted up.

Clara moved her feet to the side and kept writing.

Holly looked back and forth between the broken cologne bottle and Clara. "Are you kidding me?"

"Do I look like I'm kidding you?"

"Do your parents know?"

"They will. Tonight."

"Whoa. Remind me not to be there." Holly pulled paper towels from her bag, bent over, and talked from under the seat as she wiped. "Really, Clara, if you want my advice—"

"Thanks, but I'm way past advice."

"Well, here it is anyway." She sat back up. "Clara, you can't decline the Nicklaus. It's been announced on the news and at school and I like having a best friend that's famous and besides your parents will kill you and it's impossible for a dead person to turn down the award and why would you anyway?" She went back to wiping.

"Because I don't want to play the piano."

Holly rose up very slowly.

Clara knew Holly was looking straight at her, but she kept writing.

"It takes you three hours a day for every day of your life since before you can reach the pedals to figure this out?"

"Yes."

The bell clamored and the auditorium came alive with bustle and chatter.

Holly and Clara walked to their lockers. Holly's boyfriend joined up with them, holding on to Holly by the loop of her tight-fitting jeans.

"Hi, Holly," someone called out as the threesome passed by.

"Hey, Lisa."

"Hi, Holly."

"Hey, Smitty."

Every now and then, a "Congratulations, Clara."

Clara dropped off at her locker.

"Remember," Holly called back, already being swept downcurrent, "Nutcracker rehearsal, eight o'clock."

The Nutcracker. Clara hadn't thought about the Nutcracker in a very long time. It might be the dull, everyday world, but it felt good to be back in it.

"Pick me up?" Holly yelled from downstream.

"If I'm still alive," Clara yelled back. She propped her books and spun the lock.

Suddenly Holly was back, alone, standing beside her.

"Good luck with your parents tonight, Clara."

Clara lined the notch up with the last number and pulled the latch.

Holly kept her voice under the din. "You know, there's one thing you've taught me. About my mom. Actually."

Clara exchanged the books on the shelf for the books on her hip, waiting to find out what she could possibly have taught this very-together-in-spite-of-it-all person.

"And don't take this wrong, Clara, because I don't mean it wrong. I just mean it's true, and you made me realize. There's an advantage, of her, my mom, being gone."

Clara looked into the blue-fringed eyes.

"I never had to worry, even once, about letting her down."

The table was mostly cleared when Clara asked if they could please stay, she had something to tell them. "A story," she said, putting the "Little Daughter of the Snow" music on the table, making sure the envelope was still tucked between the pages.

Her mother was scribbling in her day-planner, her father stacking dishes in the sink. Danny stood at the open freezer door.

"It's a Russian folktale. My encore, this is the story it tells. A friend of Tashi's wrote it."

Her father sat back down. Possibly he had heard the rehearsed tone in her voice. Her mother continued scribbling but inclined her head toward Clara. Danny unwrapped an ice cream sandwich.

With her eyes fixed on the print, it seemed possible to start. "Okay. Here goes." Parents were supposed to tell stories to their children, not the other way around.

"'Long ago on the plains of Russia—'"

There was no air to make the words. She stopped, made herself breathe, and started over.

"'Long ago on the plains of Russia, there lived an old man and an old woman . . .'"

As she read, Danny came slowly back to his seat. At the top of Clara's vision, her mother reached for her father's hand on the table.

Clara's voice went up a pitch, then another, as she struggled through the story. She rushed to finish. "'And the old man and the old woman heard clearly the words of the snow girl's song, carried behind her on the wind: Old ones, old ones, I had to go, to my kin, of the snow.'"

A drop fell on the music. Clara rubbed it into the paper with her fingers. Now she could blink, let more come, and she reached for a Kleenex. From behind the tissue, she dared to look.

Her mother's face looked older than she had remembered. There were wrinkles Clara hadn't noticed before, and her skin was dry.

She couldn't see much of her father, because his free hand was rubbing his temples, blocking her view.

Danny's eyebrows were lifted. The same face as when he was putting up the free throws, before he knew Clara was there—hoping for the best, fearing the worst.

They didn't understand. Not yet. But she had wanted

them to hear the story first, before the shock that was coming turned them deaf.

Clara handed the envelope to her father. He studied the address, then took the letter out and read it. He closed his eyes for a moment, then passed it to her mother, who seemed reluctant to touch it.

As she read, her mother's eyes widened, then went back to the top of the page. They did it again. Still holding her husband's hand on the table, her fingers turned red at the tips, white at the knuckles. Finally, trembling, she passed the paper to Danny.

Danny read it, blinked up at Clara from behind his bangs, and gave it back to her.

She hadn't realized until now, but this was going to be hard on him, too. Danny, who thought, at least, that he came second. And now she was rejecting what he so desperately wanted.

"Have you shown this to Tashi?" her father asked.

Clara nodded.

"Did it kill her?" He said it matter-of-factly, not unkindly.

"Yes," Clara said finally, looking at her father. "It killed a little bit of her, I think, deep down."

"Clara," her father began again. "You may think I'm going to try to talk you out of this. And to be honest I probably would if I thought it would do any good. Because if I could talk you out of it, it would mean you hadn't given this enough thought."

He stopped to see whether Clara had anything to say, but she didn't.

"Your talent is so huge, and I think a talent like that is meant to be shared—"

"At the price of my happiness?" Clara interrupted gently.

Her father cocked his head to the side and studied her, a bewildered look on his face. "Maybe you should hold the letter, sleep on things," he said, but now his voice was different, as if he were suddenly uncertain himself. "Take some time . . ." The words trailed off. He was coming to see it. The truth.

Clara looked at her mother. Her eyes were flame blue, her lips set in a tight line.

"Please, I know this is hard," Clara offered. "But I also know it is right. It's the first thing I've known is right in a very long time."

"Did we push you, somehow, into this corner?" Her father's beautiful strong voice started to crack, and he struggled to get the words out before it broke completely. "Were we wrong, all these years?"

Clara pulled up a Kleenex and passed it to him. "No." She remembered her dad in his sunglasses, bobbing in front of the choir. She remembered her mom, the towel draped around her neck. "I just think I'm made of different . . . stuff." She wiped her tears off her cheek. "And we didn't know. Not even me, until now."

She offered another Kleenex to Danny, managing a smile through her tears. "You want in on this act, Dan?" He was always asking them to call him that, but they could never remember. He wasn't crying, but he took the Kleenex.

"Mom?" Clara held one up to her mother, wishing for any response, even a livid one.

Her mother took the tissue, folded it carefully, and pressed it against her forehead.

For a long time, they sat in a silent circle. Finally her mother reached for her day-planner. She tucked it under her arm and walked to the phone. Clara could see her at the niche in the hall, and they could all hear.

"This is Ellen Alexander, Clara Lorenzo's mother." No one who didn't know her usual businesslike tone would have detected the quaver as she dictated into the message machine. "Please call me tomorrow at work, between"—she opened the planner—"ten and ten-thirty, if possible, at the number we left. I'm afraid we need to cancel our layaway."

Clara went to the Nutcracker rehearsal, then studied in her room. Dan, as if he were trying to fill in for her, practiced string bass.

Her parents sat outside in the car. Clara peeked through the shutters often. Sometimes they were talking, sometimes they weren't. Around eleven they came in.

Before she went to bed, Clara checked on them. Her dad was in the bathroom—she could hear the water running. Her mother was in her robe on the couch, playing the tape she had made of the news clips over and over.

Clara hadn't seen the video before, and she watched intently. The red dress looked good and she gave well-spoken answers to the reporters' questions, but there was a glazed, baffled look in her eyes. She wondered if her mother saw it.

"We have to talk." Clara stepped up behind the couch.

"I can't talk." Her mother kept her eyes on the screen. "I'm afraid of what I might say."

A big wicker basket of videotapes blocked Clara's view of her mother. She picked it up off the table behind the sofa, reached over and set it down on the couch, then stood back and put her hands on her waist.

Her mother glanced at the basket and looked back at the screen. She muted the sound.

"Say it, Mother. Whatever it is. I need you to say it."

Her mother turned her head to Clara and looked straight out of the ice-blue eyes. "All right. I don't think you have the slightest idea what you are doing or why." She went back to the silent news clip.

"The folktale. Those are my reasons."

"The folktale is a farce. The folktale has nothing whatsoever to do with reality. You got that little story all twisted up in your seventeen-year-old head and you think it's profound but it's just silly and you are throwing away everything. You are ruining your life."

"One thing you got right," Clara said quietly. "*My* life."

"And you're doing a hell of a job with it."

"What else?"

"You need more?" Her mother kept her eyes on the television.

"No," Clara said calmly. "*You* need more. Because if that's your only argument, you lose."

Her mother punched the pause button, catching the girl

in the red dress with her mouth open in front of the microphones. She studied the picture for a long moment, then turned her eyes slowly back to Clara. "All right. I'll give you more." There was a millimeter's narrowing of the lids. "How could you do this to your father?"

The words kicked Clara in the gut like a well-aimed hoof.

"Yes, your father. Who generously, uncomplainingly, forfeited his life on the stage for you. Your father, with his huge voice that no one ever hears anymore."

Clara closed her eyes. "If Dad gave up singing for me, it was a mistake."

"How dare you say it was a mistake. It was love."

"Love makes mistakes—I of all people ought to know. Why do you think I put off telling you for so long? Why do you think I buried my doubts?"

Her mother turned the volume back up, but Clara raised her voice over it. "I didn't want to hurt you—but those doubts, they made me sick, real sick—inside. And if I'd gone on, it would have gone way past the folktale, Mother, way past. You're right, that folktale really doesn't have anything to do with reality. Because the reality is much worse. Because I would have been miserable, smothered, by that life you planned for me, and eventually, I think—I would have hated you for it."

She turned on her heel and was surprised to find her father standing behind her. She wondered if he had heard the part about him.

"Daddy," she said in a clear voice so that her mother would hear, "thank you for being the way you are." She squeezed his arm as she passed by.

Behind her, Clara's father spoke. "Ellen." Clara froze, her hand on the neck of the string bass. "You can have a daughter who is not a concert pianist. Or you can have a former daughter who is not a concert pianist."

The videotape went to loud static, squeaked into rewind, and started over.

She slept hard, but at 4 A.M. her screaming stomach woke her. Now that she had rested, she had the energy to replay the scene with her mother. They had both said bad things. But not untrue things, and not things that didn't need to be said. Maybe there was hope. She swore to herself to try and mend things in the morning.

It was the first time she had felt hungry in weeks, and she left the covers for the cold. Heading back from the kitchen with a stack of cinnamon toast, she glimpsed the back of her mother's head.

God. Still sitting there. But something was different.

Clara looked in, keeping her eyes on her mother's form, trying to figure out what it was that had changed. She had dimmed the lamp and turned the volume off on the video to keep from waking Clara's dad, who was asleep in the bed in the corner. Other than that she hadn't moved. It was the line of her shoulders. Before they had been squared; now they were curved.

Clara took a big breath and prayed for a fresh start. "Hi," she whispered.

"Hi."

"Whatcha doin'?"

"Watching the best moments of my life."

Mom, I'm so sorry, Clara wanted to say. So sorry. But she had to tell it better than that.

She put the toast down and moved the wicker basket—now spilling over with wadded Kleenex—aside.

Her mother looked at her. The eyes weren't flame blue or ice blue. They were a puffy, suffering blue.

Clara realized. She wouldn't be suffering unless she had accepted it. Had it been Clara's words, or her father's? Or after a hundred replayings had she finally seen the baffled look on the face of the girl in the red dress?

She put her arms around her mother. The petite frame felt thin under the heavy terrycloth. They sat there for a long time. Finally, the buttery aroma made Clara remember her stomach.

Clara unwrapped her arms and offered the plate. "Mother," she asked cautiously, "what happened between midnight and four o'clock?"

Her mother took the toast. Then she picked up the wicker basket, set it carefully on Clara's lap, and nodded toward the television.

Not until then did Clara turn and look at the screen. It was a little girl, four or five, in a cowboy hat and boots, wedged into the saddle in front of a beautiful, athletic-looking young woman with blond hair and blue eyes. One arm was snug around the little girl and held the reins, the other hand rested on her jeans in correct Western style. It was just like her mom, Clara thought, smiling to herself, to look good at everything.

The little girl's hands were sealed around the saddle horn. As Clara watched, the child turned and flashed worried brown eyes to the camera, then looked quickly back, as if she were scared she'd fall off if she didn't keep looking straight between the horse's ears.

"Was I always so serious?"

A soft smile crossed her mother's face. "Yes."

Clara remembered the weight of the basket on her lap. What was her mother trying to say, passing it to her that way?

She dug through the damp tissues down to the videos. "Clara Home from the Hospital, 3 Days Old." "Danny, First Bath." "Danny, Science Fair." "Clara, Collected Recitals." "Oregon Beach, Kites and Sand Castles."

Her mother had said she was watching the best moments of her life. Clara had thought she meant the news interviews. But she had meant these. These were what had happened between twelve and four o'clock.

"I thought Monday night was the best moment of your life," Clara said softly.

"Monday night was good." Her mother let a fresh batch of tears start down her cheeks. "But Monday night can't touch this." She nodded Clara back to the picture of the beautiful woman and the serious little girl, snugged tightly, safely, into the saddle together.

Suddenly Clara understood. She had come in to help her mother see, but her mother was making sure that Clara saw, really saw, that her mother had also chosen and what it meant. *A daughter who is not a concert pianist.* Daughter. It required two. Yes, piano was a part of who these two were—

it was one of the tapes in the basket, a part her mother would miss and a part Clara didn't think she would—but piano wasn't the biggest part, not by a long shot. And piano had nothing at all to do with "Clara Home from the Hospital, 3 Days Old." It was what Holly didn't have. No family videos. No one to let down.

Clara set the basket aside. Eyes still glued to the screen, she curled up on the couch and put her head in her mother's lap.

The camera zoomed in. The woman popped the cowboy hat off the head in front of her, unfurling long, straight hair, several shades lighter than it was now. Unaware of the video as they joggled off down the trail, the woman bent over and kissed the top of the head, caressed the hair back into place, and plopped the hat back on.

"I don't often get to kiss that lovely head anymore." It was her mother's voice, but not from the video.

Early the next morning, Clara went to see the chairman of the Nicklaus Committee. He walked her to his office with his arm around her. After Clara gave him the letter he didn't say much and had his secretary show her out.

Holly came over after school to watch the news clips. She was in the background during most of them, stationed behind Clara's shoulder. She was excited and Clara made her a copy. She would have given her the original, but she didn't think she should take anything more away from her mother.

Her father brought the *New York Times* article home. It used words like "light," "brilliant," and "clarity of style" to describe her playing. Notes and letters came, with the clipping folded inside. The AP had picked up the story, so friends and relatives were calling from all over the country. If her mom or dad answered, they handed the phone to Clara, which Clara thought was right.

The next day there was a short article in the Community section announcing the change in winners, so the committee must have put out a press release. At school, her celebrity status had worn off after the first day and nobody said anything about winning or not winning.

Clara took her music out of the Wheaties section of the bookshelves. She packed it into Danny's old camp footlocker, and he helped her drag it to the garage.

On Thursday Clara went to her piano lesson, but she didn't take her satchel.

The snow-globe was back on the ledge, the teapot was steaming, and the winter sun streamed in through the wavy glass.

Clara curled in her place on the couch. "I'd like it, Tashi, if you didn't fill my Thursday spot. At least not for a while."

Tashi poured.

"We could talk, or listen to tapes, or take a walk across the quad. Anything. Mom and Dad think it would be a good idea. And they don't mind paying."

"It sounds lovely. All except the paying part." Tashi winked over her teacup. "I do not charge for talk, my darling."

Tashi told Clara the committee chairman had called, probably only seconds after Clara had left his office. He had asked if Tashi could confirm Clara's resignation, which she had. Then he had told her that as first alternate Marshall Lawrence was the new recipient of the award and asked where he could be reached. Tashi had given him the McDonald's number.

After her talk with Tashi, Clara went down to the basement. Practice room 12 was dark, and the door swung open when she touched the knob. A piano, a bench, a light.

For days her wrist continued to bother her. She had been on a steady diet of aspirin and she knew that couldn't go on.

It didn't hurt nearly as much as it had when she played in the competition, but as time went by it didn't get any better either. She went back to the university doctor.

Her parents got a copy of the *Times's* second story, longer and with a bigger headline than the first one. Apparently declining the Nicklaus was more newsworthy than winning it. It went on at length about Marshall's performance, with no mention of a pedaling slip. It described his "round, rich tones" and his "fresh interpretation of the more romantic side" of the piece. It concluded, "Lawrence is a name to watch."

Nobody sent any articles this time. She didn't know if people didn't clip stories that began "Prestigious Piano Award Refused" or if no one knew what to say.

A bouquet of pink carnations came for her. The card just said, "Marshall." She guessed he didn't know what to say, either.

Within a week she had caught up on her school work. Her Lit paper came back with a B and "Dropped one letter grade for late turn-in" written at the top. Clara told Greg she was available to be his study partner again, but he already had a new one.

She went back to ballet class, and to Nutcracker rehearsals, which became more frequent as Christmas neared. Friday nights she went to the football games with Holly, and Saturday mornings she drove Dan—who had made second string on the middle-school team—to basketball practice. She didn't yell advice across the gym floor anymore. And ever since the night he had witnessed his sister suffer through the telling of the folktale, Dan had not, even once, called her a meathead.

Colleges were already sending brochures, and Clara talked to the school counselor about financial aid. She didn't have the talent to major in dance, but she wanted a school that at least offered ballet so she could take classes. The idea of medical school was beginning to take hold. But she was determined to explore lots of options before she made any decisions.

One night at dinner Clara's mother reported that the orchestra had started work on the New Year's program and that she was impressed with Marshall Lawrence. "A fine young man, definitely concert material," she said, looking at Clara.

"Yes," Clara said. "He is."

Dressed in blue jeans and a strapless bra, Clara squeezed between the sets of bare shoulders. It was opening night of the Nutcracker, and the rows of bulbs were hot on her skin. Three white roses had been delivered to her place at the dressing table. The petals were closed, the stems protected in small plastic water vials.

The card said, "Love to you on the night of your debut, Dad. P.S. I agree. If I had given up singing for you, it would have been a mistake." So he had heard. "But I didn't. I gave it up for me. Because I wanted to be at home with you and your mother and your unborn brother. Sometimes I miss it, but I do not regret it. I wish you the same good fortune with your choices."

Later, when Holly zipped Clara into her costume, she told her, eyes sparkling, "My dad's here!" They hugged each other tight. It was the first time Clara could remember Holly's dad coming to anything.

Because she was in the first scene, Clara was already positioned backstage when the house lights came down. "Conductor spot, stage door one," the man at the light-board said into his headphones. The auditorium hushed, and everyone waited for her mother.

The curtain was lowered, so Clara didn't see Ellen Alexander walk across the front of the orchestra and up to the podium. But she knew exactly how she did it: smiling, in a long black dress, blue eyes sparkling into the white beam that followed her, along with 3,200 heads. A bow, another wave of applause. At last it quieted and her mother cued in the overture.

Clara danced well, even with the new cast on her wrist. The costumes manager had opened the seam of a glove and taped it closed so that it didn't show from the audience.

From the stage, Clara looked for her dad and Dan and Tashi. She knew their seats were orchestra, front and center, but she couldn't see past the footlights.

Her mother, of course, was very visible, in front of Clara, in front of everyone. Once she caught Clara's eye and blew a kiss. It wasn't like her to do it because it wasn't very professional, which made it mean even more. Clara knew it wasn't the way she had dreamed of conducting her.

Back between the sets of shoulders, Clara wiped away the last smears of mascara, washed her face, and brushed out her hair. She dropped a big sweater over her warm-up leotard, and pulled on boots. When she had come in that evening, the flakes had just been starting to fall.

She zipped the card from her father into the pocket of her dance bag—maybe she'd start a new collection in the frame of her mirror. The roses she carried, being careful of the thorns.

The narrow hall was jammed with bodies, so Clara headed the opposite way. It was a short cut, a door Clara knew about because of the hours she'd spent back here playing when she was little, waiting for her mother. She was supposed to meet her family at the main stage door, where everyone else was headed, but it was quicker to go around outside than to wind through the maze of hallways. Hoping her body heat would save the flowers, she put on her coat.

A stiff wind met her as she pushed open the door under the red EXIT.

Marshall was standing under the floodlights. His cheeks were ruddy, the collar of his ski jacket turned up.

Clara looked up at the green eyes. They didn't look green in the night, but her mind filled in the exact shade.

His hands were in his pockets. "Hello, Clara."

"Marshall."

He looked at his feet and stamped the snow. "Your mother said you might come this way. I sat with your family tonight," he explained. "Your mother joined us after the performance."

So he had seen her dance.

"You're good."

"Not good enough to get a real part, I guess."

"Good enough to smile while you're up there."

It was true, she did smile when she danced.

He stamped the snow some more, and looked around.

She tugged her coat tighter and looked around in the other direction.

"So," he asked, "what have you been doing with yourself?"

"School. Ballet."

"Any piano?"

"No."

He hesitated. "Ever?"

"I don't know."

He blinked but said nothing. It reminded Clara of the time she had blinked when the doctor examined her wrist.

"What have you been up to?" she asked.

"Some rehearsing already." He had tramped the snow down, clear through to the frozen mud. "My parents are driving up for the concert, bringing my sisters."

"After that?"

"Go home. Maybe take some classes at UT. Orientation at Juilliard starts the first of September. It seems like an impossible time to wait." He pushed the toe of his tennis shoe into a ridge of frozen mud. "What's next for you?"

"Be a regular person my senior year."

He looked straight at her. "You won't ever be a regular person, Clara, no matter what you do. Not to me."

"Thank you, Marshall." She sighed. "And Tashi's invited me to go to Russia with her next summer."

"I heard. That'll be good."

"Yeah, that'll be good." Clara pulled her coat tighter.

Marshall stuffed his hands deeper into his pockets. "How is your wrist?"

She opened her coat and held up her injured hand, remembering the time she had done it at McDonald's. "I'm in a cast for six weeks. I rebroke it."

"Rebroke?"

"There was a fracture that didn't show up on the x-rays the first time. It was weak. And I rebroke it. Maybe during the finals. Maybe—earlier." She added, "Maybe playing the Rachmaninoff."

Did he understand that she would have played the Rachmaninoff for him that day even if she had known she was breaking her wrist? She wanted him to understand that.

"You competed with a broken wrist?"

"Marshall, that wasn't the hardest part of it. You must know that."

They looked at each other.

"Clara—" he blurted, "I came here to ask you something."

"Okay."

He squared his shoulders and took in a deep breath, but the question came out weakly. "Why?"

Now Clara stamped the snow. "Marshall, would you like to go somewhere, somewhere warm, and sit down maybe? We could talk, drink some coffee, you know, and I—I will try, really try, to tell you."

He said nothing. He just looked at her.

Clara's chest ached. She held herself together.

"Why, Clara?"

After a very long moment, she spoke slowly. "Marshall. I could imagine my life without it."

He closed his eyes, and his head fell back. A long, steamy breath escaped. When he tipped his head forward again, his eyes were still closed. Snowflakes dotted his lashes. His features looked looser than they had before.

It was a bold thing to do, but she couldn't not do it. She reached up and pressed her fingers to his face.

His cheek was just barely rough, like sand, the way it had been against her cheek that once, the way she had thought it would be that very first day by the bulletin board—why was she thinking of sand castles, standing here in the cold?—but he didn't reach up and take her hand and kiss it and hold it the way he was supposed to. All he did was open his eyes.

She took her hand away.

Silence loomed.

"Marshall, I'm sorry it meant you had to win this way—"

"Listen, Clara, I'll take my shot. It's better than not winning. And I was so scared, so scared—"

"I know."

"—that you had done it, you know—"

"I know."

"—for me."

"No."

Silence again. Clara looked up into the floodlight, where the flakes swirled under the beam.

"Marshall, I really am the same person. I think I am a better person, even, in a way."

He swallowed. "Clara, I—I—respect your decision, but—"

If he would only reach for her hair, tuck it back behind her shoulder, then he'd see, he'd remember, what she felt like, that he still loved her. Clara willed his hand toward her. His arm moved a fraction, but he stopped it.

"But—I don't think I can love you, this way—" His voice broke. "If you don't play."

Cold, cold air filled her lungs. He was in love with a girl who played. Really played. And that girl didn't exist anymore.

She opened her coat and took out one of the roses, tucking the remaining pair back inside. She put the bud into his big, perfect hand. "Thank you for the flowers you sent." The winter air was too much. The stem already drooped.

"I should have called or come by," he said.

Yes, you should have.

Marshall dusted the snow from his shoulders. He dusted them again. "It's cold."

She pulled her coat back tight around her. "Pretty cold."

"Well."

"Well."

"Everyone's waiting for us."

He took the first step. They walked side by side, but with a space between, along the back of the building. He didn't take her dance bag off her shoulder and put it on his. He didn't put his arm around her and hold her tight against him.

Around the corner and down the length of the building, a crowd would be huddled. Clara's parents and brother and teacher and friend would be among them, camped around the main door, chattering as they waited with hugs and congratulations, oblivious to the freezing temperature. But here, the world was hushed and empty.

Clara looked out into the night. The snow was coming thick now, already drifting against the few cars left in the parking lot, which was covered—a still, frozen lake. Their footfalls made no sound. It was beautiful, she thought, the way the snow changed busy, noisy things into still, quiet ones.

Marshall looked over at her and smiled. "Do you think there'll be a white Christmas?"

She smiled back at him, remembering that he liked the song. But there were five days left before then, and the snow almost never lasted that long.

Stepping closer, she put her arm firmly around his waist. "I think, Marshall, that the snow might last. But I also think that some things—" Snowfalls, and cut flowers, and music in the air. Sand castles, too, she realized, belonged on the list. "Some things are precious because they don't."

They stopped and faced each other.

He reached out and tucked her hair back, once on the left, once on the right. She put her hand on his rough cheek, and he bent toward her, and his breath was warm on her ear and he kissed the top of it, and she could feel him breathing in the fragrance of her shampoo. She wished he would kiss her again, and it was almost possible that he might because he lingered. But she knew that he wouldn't.

They straightened and moved apart.

Behind them, their footprints were already filling. Ahead, the snow was perfect and untouched. He offered his arm and she took it, and they walked together around the corner.